TIGHTROPE

Book Two

MADDIE WADE

Tightrope
Book Two
By Maddie Wade

Published by Maddie Wade
Copyright © July 2018 Maddie Wade

Cover: Envy Creative Designs
Editing: Black Opal Editing
Formatting: Black Opal Editing

ACKNOWLEDGMENTS

Thank you to Linda and Black Opal Editing. You have become so much more than my editor. Your friendship and honesty mean so much and helps me to be able to put out the best book I can.

Huge thanks you to my beta readers, Greta, Becky D, Clem and Maria for helping me guide this story to the conclusion I wanted.

To Charlene at Envy Designs, thank you for the gorgeous cover, you never get it wrong.

To the readers and reviewers and bloggers of Itsy Bitsy Promotions, thank you for your support. I hope this book is a satisfying conclusion and doesn't leave you swearing at me. The reviews you leave are all welcome and so appreciated, I read every single one with a smile on my face.

My readers, you are why I do this. Your thirst for what I write keeps me typing and working to put out the stories you want to read.

This book is dedicated to Clem, you are always there for me when I need you. You are my sister, my friend, and my confidant.

CHAPTER ONE

LEXI

I CAN HEAR A COMMOTION, DEEP UNKNOWN VOICES yelling at each other, and wish they would just shut the hell up so I can sleep.

"She's coming around," a woman's voice says as I struggle to shrug off the fog that shrouds my brain. Opening my eyes, I see a sea of faces looking at me. Putting my hand out behind me, I try to push up but a gentle hand on my shoulder eases me back.

"Just stay still, Miss. I have someone calling an ambulance." I instantly remember why I'm here, and the pain in my chest intensifies.

Hunter has let me down too. Blinking back tears, I focus on the man who is looking at me. He is tall, with gray hair, tanned weathered skin, and warm brown eyes. The lines near the edges showing he smiled often.

"No," I snap a little too sharply. The wounded look on the kind older gentleman's face makes me wince. "I mean I'm fine. I just need to get back to my friend, she's downstairs in the parking lot." I see the man who had confronted me, breaking my heart, and shattering any hope I had left, pacing at the back of the reception area. His phone is glued to his ear as he has a very heated conversation with someone.

The older man indicates the security guard who is hovering nearby to go and find Cherry. He has no idea what she looks like, but Cherry is sure to make herself known.

"You really should be checked out by a doctor, my dear," the older man says as he and the receptionist help me to a low sectional couch. He is wearing what looks like a custom suit, so whoever he is, he has money.

No, I need to get the hell out of here so that I can have a melt-down in private.

"I'm fine. I just need to rest and maybe become a nun or something," I grumble. The receptionist hands me a glass of water with a smile. Her demeanor is much more helpful now that the boss is watching. Smiling, I sip the water, letting the cool liquid soothe the pain from the tears that I force away.

"Thank you," I say, giving the glass back to the girl. The older man sits beside me, a look of concern on his face. "Are you sure I can't call an ambulance? You look very pale, my dear."

Shaking my head, I answer him, my voice calm and clear. "No. Honestly, I just need to go home."

The younger man moves closer, standing in front of us. "It's already left," he says to the man at my side and I watch with fascination as the air around the older guy becomes electric.

Standing up he confronts the young guy. "Then see that my son gets the message as soon as he lands," he growls and gone is the kind distinguished man. In his place is a force of nature—a man you did not cross.

"Yes, of course, Mr. McKenzie," the other man says with forced politeness, his jaw rigid with tension.

I look between the two men as the dawning realization hits. *Mr. McKenzie? Oh, God, is this Hunter's father?* I need to leave before he realizes why I'm here and who I am. I have no clue if Hunter has told his family the details but if he's moved on I'm sure as hell not going to stick around and make nice with his family.

Standing quickly, I wobble as dizziness strikes. Reaching out I grab the nearest object, which happens to be Mr. McKenzie's arm. He steadies me with a hand on my back.

"Please, Miss. You need to sit," he says as he eases me back down, his eyes wandering over the barely concealed bruises on my face, but he is too polite to mention them. I look at the other man, guessing that he is a friend of Hunter's and probably he thinks I'm the devil and catch the slight look of worry and indecision that passes over his face.

I'm about to reply when the door flies open and Cherry blows in like a hurricane.

Rushing to my side she drops onto her knees beside me. "Honey, are you okay? What did that asshole say to you? I'm going to kick his ass," she says before taking a breath.

I try not to laugh as I look at my friend, who has taken my hand. She looks like a furious avenging pixie in a pink flowered skirt and white peasant blouse.

My hand snakes out and holds on to Cherry tightly, needing the contact. My friend is always my port in a storm it seems. "I'm fine. Cherry can we just get out of here please," I implore as I allow her to search my face.

"Of course we can sweetie." Cherry looks up as she goes to stand, and I watch in fascination as she and the handsome younger man look at each other. First shock and then hatred cross her pretty features. "You!"

"You!" both Cherry and the man say at the same time as they see each other.

Ignoring the man, Cherry turns back to me and helps me gently to my feet. "Come on, Lex. Let's get you out of here. I don't like the smell in here," Cherry says as she maneuveres me toward the door.

"Cherry hang on," the man says from behind us.

I feel Cherry go stiff before she whirls on the man. "No, Jake, I won't hang on. I should have known you were involved. Hurting women is what you do right," she spits as she turns to leave again.

"Lexi." Hunter's father stops me with a firm hand on my arm. "Here is my number. If you need anything, please call me. I have a feeling there has been a huge misunderstanding between you and my son. Despite everything you have heard and seen this morning, Hunter is a good man and he cares about you a great deal."

I search his face and find no malice, just pure honesty. How had Hunter turned out to be so cold when he had this man for a father?

Inclining my head, I smile a sad smile. "Thank you, Mr. McKenzie, but I think Hunter has made it clear what he wants, and I will respect that. I won't stop him from seeing his son if he wants to, but I won't contact him again either. I'm afraid I'm all out of energy where men are concerned." I take the card and he nods his understanding.

Regret fills me, he seems like such a kind man, now I won't ever get the chance to find out.

Following along beside Cherry we make it to the elevator, the tension in my friend's body shocking me. Cherry is the most chilled person I know, besides Frankie. Stepping inside, Cherry presses the button for the ground floor. As the door shuts, a suited hand shoots out to stop them from closing. Jake steps in, his hair now tousled as if he has been running his hands through it, the look on his face is flustered and unsure, which makes me smile.

Cherry studiously ignores him as he presses the button for the ground floor.

"Cherry I—" he never finishes the sentence.

My little fairy friend rounds on him. Pointing her finger in his chest she pokes it. "No, you don't get to speak to me. You are nothing but a lowlife, lying asshole. Stay away from me and stay away from my friend or you won't like what I do," she snarls.

I try to cover the surprise I feel at her angry tirade. I have no idea who Jake is to her or what he has done, but I'm going to find out the first chance I get.

"Me? I'm a liar? You're the one who promised me forever and then left, not the other way around, Blossom."

Cherry looks like her head is going to explode, her jaw tight, her face red, her breath heaving. "Fuck you, Jake. You can't even be honest with yourself and don't call me that," she growls as she turns back to face the elevator doors.

Jake is so intent on Cherry that I'm able to look at him without him knowing. He is very handsome, in a playboy kind of way, not dark and mysterious like Hunter, but still drop-dead gorgeous. I wonder if it is a job requirement. *Must be fit and drop-dead handsome.* The myriad of emotions flash over his arrogant, handsome face as he looks at Cherry makes me wonder if I have pegged him wrong.

"If I recall, *Blossom*," he says with emphasis on the Blossom, "you loved me calling you that. Admit it, even now you're wet for me," he ends with an assured smile.

Oh no! I have no idea what is happening, but I know my friend and he has just pushed her too far. He glances at me as I draw in a sharp breath and doesn't see the right hook she swings at him, landing a solid punch to his face. He grabs his face just as the doors to the lobby open. I follow Cherry as she marches out at a rapid rate, dragging me by the arm. I grin for a second, feeling much better, pleased that for once the drama wasn't mine. I twist to look back and see Jake watching with a smirk as he exits the elevator behind us.

CHAPTER TWO

LEXI

WE SIT IN SILENCE AS CHERRY DRIVES US TOWARD THE shop. Despite fainting, I feel physically okay. A call to the doctor reassures me that it is normal as my blood pressure is erring on the low side. He tells me to rest and make sure I drink enough fluids.

The only fluids I want right now are alcohol, but as I rub my bump I know it will all be worth it, so I get Cherry to stop at the store and get some ice-cream. I turn to look at my friend who hasn't said a word about what happened.

"Stop looking at me," she says as she chances a quick glance my way.

"No," I laugh trying to take my mind off my broken heart.

"He and I had a fling back in college and it ended badly. That's all there is to it and I don't want to talk about it anymore." Cherry says as she parks in front of our beautiful store. Even now, after all the heartache and pain, seeing our shop and the business we have built gives me a thrill.

"Why didn't you tell me about him?" I ask softly once we're inside, with a spoon each in the ice-cream tubs.

Cherry looks at me and her normal sunny personality seems dulled. "Nothing to say. I thought he was great and he turned out to be a jerk. When I came home I just wanted to forget and I still do. Please, can we not talk about him?"

I search her face and the desperation in her voice persuades me that she doesn't want to talk about him, so I nod.

"Okay, sweetie."

Relief washes over her features before she replaces it with a smile. "Tell me what happened with Hunter."

The pain hits me in the sternum as I think about the blow Jake had delivered. "He left for China with his new fiancee according to Jake." I set the ice-cream aside as the sick feeling in my stomach increases.

"Oh, honey, I'm so sorry." She embraces me, and I let her. The familiar scent of her perfume settling me a little. But I don't cry, tears won't come. I feel numb as if I have nothing left to give, my heart so closed from all the blows it has suffered that I didn't think it would ever recover.

"Me too, but at least I know now. From now on it's me and my baby against the world. Men aren't worth it, at least not the ones I meet."

"You have your friends too," Cherry says as I pull away. I can feel myself pulling away emotionally from everyone and everything. My ability to trust myself is gone.

"I know. I love you all. I just want to move forward as if none of the last six months have happened." A kick to my stomach reminds me that isn't possible.

"How about we go shopping for clothes for this guy tomorrow?" she suggests.

"Sounds good. I need to stock up on some more stuff for him."

Cherry and I spend the rest of the afternoon working. We are both trying to catch up after missing work this morning. I have finished the drawing for a dressing table and decide to take a file for a new project home. Keeping busy will be the key and I also need to try and get ahead so I have more time when my son is born.

Whatever happens, I won't think about Hunter or Dean. If I do, I'm worried that I won't survive the onslaught of emotions that will ensue.

CHAPTER THREE

HUNTER

THE FLIGHT HAS BEEN HELL AND I'VE BURIED MYSELF IN work to stop myself from thinking about Lexi. Lola has been clingy and gushing the whole flight trying to get my attention by rubbing against me. I'd never noticed it before but now every little thing she does annoys me. Her voice is too whiny, her laugh is too fake, the way she nibbles at a piece of lettuce as if that will sustain her. I find myself comparing everything she does to Lexi and each time she comes out a sad second.

It doesn't seem to matter that she has lied, that she is married, that her baby isn't mine. All that matters is the way she made me feel, as if I was the center of her world. She looked at me with so much trust, every word I spoke she heard. Not because I was rich, not because I was the boss or the person the media portrayes but because she truly wanted to hear what I had to say.

Walking into the Fairmont Hotel in Beijing we are greeted by the hotel staff ready to take our luggage. The clip-clop of Lola's heels as she runs to keep up with me is grating on my nerves.

"Hold on, Hunter," she laughs as she takes my arm.

I grind my teeth in an effort not to snap at her. Who the fuck wears shoes like that for long-haul flight? I smile and keep my mouth zipped as she hangs on my arm. I know I'm being a dick, I asked her to come and now I realize what a mistake it was. No matter what happened with Lexi and me, it is not fair to drag someone else into this shit show.

After we are checked in I turn to hand Lola her key card and see her face fall.

"We could share a room, Hunter. It's not like we haven't before," she says as she flutters her perfectly lined eyelashes at me. I look at her for a second, wanting my body to respond to her but there is nothing, not a single twitch.

"No, that won't be necessary. Let's keep this professional, Lola. We have a lot to get done on this trip."

Her back snaps straight and I can see she is irritated by my lack of response to her. She obviously saw this as a sign and if it hadn't been for a certain blue haired goddess, it might have been. "If that's what you want, Hunter," she replies primly.

"It is," I reply and turn and walk to the elevator without waiting for her. She would either follow or she wouldn't.

We stand in silence as we reach the top floor.

"Will you need anything else this evening?"

"No, thank you," I answer to soften the harsh reply.

Lola nods and I know I need to send her home. Even though I want a family, having one with just anyone is a mistake. I see that now that I've had a chance to put some space between me and my feelings of betrayal.

Closing my door, I dump my bags in the bedroom barely taking in the plush interior or the extravagant décor. I move to the bar and grab a whiskey, tipping two fingers into the cut crystal glass and taking a swallow. The burn hits my stomach and it feels good.

Taking out my phone I see I have eight missed calls form Jake and two from my father. Jake's calls are not unusual, but my fathers are. Worry that something has happened to him or my mother worms its way into my gut as I hit call on the phone.

I walk to the couch and drop down with a sigh as I listen to it ring. Beijing is twelve hours behind home, so it's now close to midnight there, but with the need to know and the feeling that something profound has happened burning in me, I wait for dad to answer.

"Hello, son."

My instant reaction is relief that he is okay followed by worry as his voice sounds off somehow—tired. "Dad is everything okay?" I ask as I sit forward balancing my elbows on my knees, letting the glass in my hand hang between my legs.

"We had a visitor at the office today, Hunter."

The way he says it makes my stomach churn in apprehension. "And?"

"It was Lexi. I'm not sure what is going on, son, but her face was black and blue. It looked like she had been badly beaten."

I battle the urge to vomit as nausea rushes up my throat at the thought of Lexi hurt. My hand shakes so much I have to put the glass down as whiskey spills down it.

"What happened?"

I hear a tired sigh on the other end of the call and I know this has upset my father. "I don't know, she didn't say. She was asking for you and Jake told her you had gone to China with your fiancée. She took it pretty hard and fainted. I wanted to call an ambulance, but she wouldn't let me. I don't know what is going on, son, but the woman I met did not strike me as the type of person to cheat and do all the things you believe she has."

"Fucking hell," I curse as I throw the glass across the room in anger. "Jake had no right to say that to her."

"I know, but he thought he was protecting you. He seemed pretty upset when she fainted and is feeling bad about it now," my father replies, ever the peacemaker.

"Did she say what she wanted?"

"No, but she is pretty adamant that the baby is yours. Is it possible you got it wrong? Who told you it wasn't your baby?"

"Her husband." Even as I say the words I realize what a total idiot I have been. Of course, he would say that if he still wanted her. I should have spoken to Lexi, been more forceful about seeing her and hearing it from her.

"Um, well maybe you should have heard it from her. Whatever has happened to that poor girl is bad. I'll stay in touch and try and keep an eye out for her because, God knows, it looks like she needs someone in her corner."

My father has a way of censuring me and showing his displeasure without actually saying it. The fact that he was disappointed in me made me feel like shit. Worry about Lexi fills my blood and the urge to catch the first flight home has me itching to get off the phone and get a cab to the airport.

"Tell Jake he needs to get his ass to Beijing, I'm coming home."

"No need, son, he's already on his way."

I hang my head as relief hits me. If I was half the man one day my dad is now, I would be happy.

"Thank you."

"Don't thank me yet, son. I think you have an uphill battle on your hands with this, and Hunter?"

"Yes, dad?"

"If you are not all in with this then please leave this poor girl alone. I have a feeling she is reaching the end of what she can cope with."

"I understand." And I did. Even if everything Dean had said was true, I needed Lexi to know I was there for her. A niggling feeling told me I'd fucked up huge when I walked away. We hung up after a few more words were exchanged.

I dial the front desk and ask them to book me on the first flight to the US. I then dial Lola's room.

"Hello?"

"Lola it's Hunter. I just want to let you know that there has been a change of plans and I'm returning to the States. Jake is flying in to replace me."

"Is everything okay?" she asks with genuine concern.

"Yes, I just have some personal stuff to take care of."

"Oh, okay. Do you want me to stay and help Jake?"

"Would you mind?"

"No, of course not. It will be nice to be useful."

Lola was not a bad person, I just didn't love her. She didn't deserve a life with a man who didn't love her.

"Thank you."

I open my laptop and take out my computer. Logging into my old social media and re-instating my email account

I realize how selfish I have been to take away all avenues of communication from Lexi. I had been hurt but it was no excuse. Logging into my inbox my heart stops when I see an email from her.

With a shaking hand, I click it open.

DEAR HUNTER,

I DON'T KNOW *how to start this email except with an apology. I did not receive the email to meet you. My life has been a living nightmare these last few days. When I got home from the hospital with Dean, I found out some things about him that resulted in a confrontation. He turned violent and attacked me. I heard you knock on the door, but I couldn't get to you. He knocked me unconscious after holding me down and waiting for you to leave.*

When I came to I was alone, so I called Cherry and was taken to the hospital. I got home tonight and decided to check my email. Somehow it seems he has been into my home again, as I found the email from you in the trash folder.

I don't know what Dean told you about me, but I can tell you this—the child I carry is your son. He was conceived in passion. For me, he will be born to a mother who is desperately in love with his father.

This may be too much for you, but it's true. I love you with all my heart. You have made me feel like 'me' again, the very best version of me. I hope you will give me a chance to explain everything that has happened and forgive me for not meeting you.

YOURS ALWAYS,
Lexi xx

. . .

FURY HAS me clenching my fists and pacing the room. That motherfucker had attacked her, hurt her, and I had been close enough to stop it. Shame hits me and I almost double up with it. I could have stopped all this, but my adolescent sulking had allowed the woman I love to get hurt and my child—my son—to be put in danger.

Punching the wall so hard it puts a dent in the drywall, I feel no relief except the pain in my knuckles which serves no purpose. I want to pummel that bastard until he is bloody and bleeding. *Attacking a fucking pregnant woman.* I would bury him if it was the last thing I did.

But first I had to get to Lexi and beg her to forgive me.

CHAPTER FOUR

LEXI

I grumbled the entire way to the doctors' office, but the truth is, it's a relief to get the all-clear after my fainting spell. I've been prescribed some iron tablets as my blood test came back that my hemoglobin was a little on the low side. Which accounted for my fainting spell.

"Do you want to come and see Frankie with me?" Cherry asks as we get in the car. Frankie and I have chatted on the phone and he reassured me he was fine but worried about me. I hadn't seen him since the attack on either of us and really want to visit him, just to see for myself he is okay.

The police have double checked the CCTV footage and found some grainy images of a man a few blocks away that fitted the description of the person who had attacked Frankie. They were trying to clean them up to see if they could get a clear ID on him. Something kept niggling me about the timing of his attack, despite what Dean had done to me, was it a stretch to think he may have attacked my friend? I didn't know, and it was driving me crazy.

"No, I want to leave it a few days until my face heals a bit more first." The bruises were turning an ugly shade of green now making them look even worse than before. Cherry nods and pulls away from the curb. I watch the scenery pass me by as we drive in comfortable silence.

I feel hollow since my visit to Hunter's offices two days ago. No pain, no tears, just empty, dead, and tired. Cherry was worried, I could tell by the way she was hovering all the time. I tried to tell her I was okay, but she knows me better than I know myself. I just can't allow myself to feel anymore and I don't have the energy either.

I have reached a limit of what I can handle so I put the brakes on and stopped myself from feeling anything. I know there will be a payday coming when this hits me, but I need some time to gather my physical strength before I let it happen.

As we round the turn onto my road I see a fancy, dark gray sedan parked at the curb. I lean forward in my seat as we pass it trying to figure out who it is.

"Who is that?" Cherry asks as we drive past, pulling into my drive.

"No idea," I say shaking my head. "Probably the realtor," I guess. I hope it isn't the police. I just don't have it in me right now to deal with them.

"Do you want me to stay?" Cherry asks as I grab the handle to open the door. I swivel back to my friend. She has been my rock these last few weeks, but I need to stand on my own two feet. I will be having my son in a few months and I need to show him I'm strong.

Reaching out I take her hand in mine. "No thanks, sweetie. I can manage with whatever this is. Anyway, all this pink is making my eyes bleed." I laugh as she squints a glare at me.

"Fine, me and my extraordinary dress sense will leave you to your mundane drab existence."

I laugh as I exit the car, watching as she reverses out onto the road. I wait while the car door of the gray sedan swings open. I inhale sharply as I watch Hunter's father get out of the car. For a second, I panic and consider calling Cherry to come back. But then I remember my vow to my unborn son and straighten my spine. He has probably come to tell me to stay away from his son. Well, he doesn't have to worry, I have no intention of contacting him.

He has a relaxed gait as he approaches me, a closed expression on his still handsome face. Despite the casual chinos and the pale green sweater, he still looks every inch the tycoon that he was. The air around him seems to realize that when this man spoke, you listened.

"Lexi," he says as he comes to a stop a few feet from me.

"Hello, Mr. McKenzie," I reply.

His eyes travel over my face and I see the slight wince on his face. I hadn't worn a lot of makeup today— the doctor has seen it all before and I wasn't going anywhere after so didn't see the point. I struggle with the need to drop my head, hiding my face and the ugly bruises from him. Shame fills me, but I fight it back. This wasn't my doing. I raise my face and look him dead in the eye.

I see an expression of what looks like pride cross his face, but it is fleeting. I miss moments like this with my owns parents. They spend so much time in Greece, and it means I don't see them as often as I'd like to. But at the moment, it was a good thing. They are already worried sick without seeing the state I'm in.

"I'm sorry to just stop by like this but do you have a few minutes?" He looks earnest and sincere as he faces me unblinking.

I tilt my head as I consider his request. What could he possibly have to say to me? But then I remember his kindness when I'd fainted and relent.

I wasn't an idiot though and despite the fact he seems nice, I didn't know this man—not really.

"Would you like to take a walk to the park down the road?" I ask motioning to the park with my head. It would be full of moms with kids and much safer than going into my empty house.

"Yes, of course, that sounds perfect."

I walk toward him, and we head slowly toward the park, each lost in thoughts of what we want to say. I decide to let him go first as he'd come looking for me not the other way around.

"I used to bring Hunter to the park all the time when he was a kid," he starts wistfully. "He loved the climbing bars. He would stand at the top and shout for me to watch him. Damn near gave me a heart attack every time."

We reach the park and take a seat on the bench. The sounds of children playing and people laughing calm my nerves.

"I guess kids have to be kids. I can only imagine how hard it is. I know I'm going to want to wrap this one up in cotton wool when he's born," I say as I caress my bump, looking across at the bars and trying so hard not to imagine Hunter with our son just as his father had described.

"A son?"

I look at him with a smile I can't contain. "Yes. I found out I'm having a son, Mr. McKenzie," I reply.

"Please call me Hank," he says with a smile. "Well, a son will certainly keep you on your toes, but honestly my dear there is no greater joy than a child." He looks lost in time as he speaks as if he sees images of the past playing out in front of him.

"I know. It's a shame not everyone agrees with that," I say trying to hide the pain and bitterness I feel.

Hank looks at me with a soft expression on his face. "Lexi, I don't know what happened between you and my son, but I know this, he cares about you deeply and he will be a good father."

"I agree that one day he will be a good father, but he doesn't believe the child I carry is his. My ex-husband managed to convince him it was his child and now he's shut me out because of it. I tried to get hold of him, but he closed his email accounts and then when I came to his office..." I throw my hand up in frustration. "Well, you know what happened. I found out he moved on, so I'm afraid I don't see how he can care about me if he could do that."

Hank turns toward me taking my hand in a fatherly gesture that makes my throat clog. "Lexi, he is not engaged to Lola. He was hurting and reacted very badly. I'm not trying to excuse him, but he's a good man. Give him some time and I'm sure he'll come around."

"That's just it, it's all such a mess I don't think he will," I say on a sob.

Hank pulls me into a hug as I let the tears come. I tell him everything. Dean's stroke, what he had said to me, meeting Hunter—although I leave out some of the details.

How Hunter had found me, how I had fallen in love with him. Everything. I didn't leave anything out.

"So, you see, it is all a big mess. I don't have the time or the energy to give to Hunter and why would he want to get involved with me even if he didn't know that? What man in his right mind would want that baggage?" I ask as I pull away and take the handkerchief he gives me. I wipe my eyes and nose and hold the scrunched-up cloth in my hand as I look at the children playing.

"When my wife and I had been married for three years, I found out she'd had an affair with a colleague of mine. We worked it out and we have a better marriage than ever. But that affair resulted in Hunter. Not a day has gone by when I haven't been grateful that he is here, that I got to be his father. That boy is the very best of me and his mother and I love him with all my heart. But Hunter found out about his conception about five years ago and has never really forgiven his mother for it."

Hank looks down at his hands as I listen in earnest. "Their relationship has always been tough but that made it worse. It breaks her heart and mine to see how he battles for something he didn't do. My point is, he has an extremely strong reaction to what he sees as betrayal, and he also has guilt for something that isn't his fault. As much as I think he has behaved badly, I understand why he did. When he sat in front of me and told me about you and this situation, he asked me if I could forgive him."

Hank shakes his head sadly. "He blames himself not you, and on some level, he's trying to protect himself from getting hurt. Because you my dear, have the power to hurt him like nobody ever has and it terrifies him."

"I understand all that, but it doesn't change the fact that he isn't here, and he didn't give me the chance to have my say," I answer even though my heart hurts for Hunter and his dad.

"I know, but you need to stop blaming yourself too. I see you fighting against what you feel and what you think you should feel. I'm not saying you should forgive him, but please for the sake of my grandson, give him a chance to try to make it up to you."

"Wow, that was a cheap shot."

"I didn't say I wouldn't play dirty if it means two people who are in love get to see the error of their ways." He smiles as he speaks, taking the edge off his words.

We sit in silence for a few minutes just watching the world go by and thinking about what has been said.

"Shall we get an ice-cream?" Hank asks as he points to the ice-cream parlor on the other side of the park.

"Sure, why not? I'm fat anyway," I laugh as I slip my arm into his.

"Blooming is the word you're looking for my dear," he replies with a smile. We chat about other things as we eat. My shop, his company, his daughter and granddaughter. It is lovely and relaxed, and I can see that despite Hunter not being his biological son, he was very much like him.

As we walk back to his car I tell him so. "Hunter is very much like you, you have the same caring nature."

We stop at my front door.

"Does that mean you will give him a chance?"

"Well, he isn't here so I don't know that it matters, but I will never come between Hunter and his son and I won't stop you or your family from having contact either. That's all I can promise at this point, Hank," I say.

He nods and kisses my cheek. "That is all I ask."

I wave as he drives away after I promise to keep in touch and become his friend on Facebook which makes me laugh. Hank is a good man and clearly loves his son. I'm not sure I'll ever trust Hunter again, but one thing is certain. I won't stop my son from getting to know him. It's funny, I still feel numb, but the dead feeling has lifted.

Now while I still miss Hunter, the pain is less.

CHAPTER FIVE

LEXI

MY HOUSE SMELLS AMAZING, I'M MAKING SLUTTY brownies. The combination of cookie dough and brownie is heavenly, especially as I add salted caramel in between the layers. They are literally a heart attack on a plate. My cholesterol is going through the roof just looking at them and I don't give a fuck.

It is my way of giving another fuck you to my ex. The last few years my home had been a temple to all things healthy and now I'm eating what I want, when I want. So, the fact that because I slept all afternoon now means that I'm baking at ten at night doesn't matter to anyone but me.

I talked to Cherry about Hanks visit and the things he had said, I thought she would be very much against me having anything to do with Hunter if he ever did show up again, but she hadn't been and said she agreed with Hank and his take on why Hunter had reacted the way he did.

Thoughts of Hunter are what's keeping me up, well

that and heartburn. It's strange the things people don't warn you about pregnancy, heartburn and leaky boobs being two of them.

Taking the oven mitt, I open the oven and test the brownies. They are still lovely and gooey, so I take them out and place the tray on a wire rack to cool. I notice the music I had been playing has stopped so I move through the kitchen to the living room and stop short when I see a shadow move past the window.

My heart starts to beat fast as fear grips me. I hate that I am now terrified of the man who had shared so much of my life with me. Walking backward I grab the phone from the side and am about to call the police when the doorbells rings. I pause, looking at the door, my finger on the buttons of the phone. Surely Dean wouldn't be silly enough to ring the doorbell? Would he?

Moving slowly as if they can somehow see through the door, I stand on the other side and wait. It rings again, and someone knocks.

"Lexi, please open up."

My hand flies to my chest in shock at the sound of Hunter's voice on the other side. I lean up and look through the peephole and sure enough there he is looking disheveled and delicious on the other side. I take a breath to calm my racing heart, which is now racing for another reason rather than fear.

Unlocking the door, I pull it open a fraction but not enough to invite him in. He spins around and the sight of him is more than I can take. He is so handsome he takes my breath away. Just seeing him makes me want to throw away all my vows to keep him away, but then I remember the pain he has caused me, and I shut it down.

Despite how much Dean has hurt me both mentally

and physically, Hunter has hurt me ten times more. He was the one for me, the one who could make my life complete, but he was also the one who could destroy me like Dean never had the power to do.

"Hunter! What are you doing here?"

He pushes a hand through his hair as he looks at me. His eyes move over the now faded bruises on my face down to the bump where our son is kicking me. He looks tired, haggard even. His eyes are slightly bloodshot, his skin is not the vibrant healthy color it normally is.

"Can I come in and talk to you for a few minutes? I promise I won't take up much of your time."

I consider his request and the low, soft, almost pleading way he has asked and relent. He deserves the right to explain and he was my child's father. After all, we would need to be civil to one another for at least the next eighteen years.

I swing the door open and move back out of the way, not wanting him to touch me, knowing that I'm not strong when it comes to him. Just the smell of his shower gel and something that is uniquely Hunter almost brings me to my knees as he sweeps past me. I have somehow forgotten in the last few weeks how he can dominate a space without even trying. He stands in the entrance, looking around as if he's uncertain what to do. I have never seen Hunter unsure of anything and it makes me sad.

"Have you been baking?" he asks as he lifts his head to sniff.

I smile and nod as I move past him to the kitchen, hoping he gets the hint and follows.

"I have. I made slutty brownies," I say as I move to the cooling tray and start to cut the slab into smaller pieces.

"Would you like some?" I ask partly out of politeness and partly because I'm going to have some.

He rubs his hands together as he looks around at the new cameras and alarms I had in the house. His jaw clenches, and I know he is angry. His eyes cut to me and he smiles. *Oh God, why did he do that?* I am defenseless against this man's charm.

"Yes, please. Do you need some help?"

"You can pass me the ice-cream from the freezer if you don't mind." I put a piece in two bowls and scoop out the ice-cream Hunter hands me. It starts to melt off the still warm and gooey brownie as soon as it touches the bowl. I hand him a bowl as he takes a seat at the island with me.

I dig my spoon in and take a big piece of brownie and ice-cream, before popping it into my mouth.

"Oh, that's so good," I mouth around the decadent sweetness. I look up as Hunter chuckles, his warm eyes hitting me.

"Is making sex noises when you eat a new pregnancy symptom?" he asks with a grin.

"Haha, just try it clever ass and you will see what I mean."

I watch him open his mouth and take a bite of the brownie. His eyes close on a long blink before he opens them again.

"So good," he says his mouth half full.

I smirk, and we continue to eat in silence until both our bowls are empty.

When we are done I take the bowls to the sink and rinse them before loading them into the dishwasher. I can't put this off any longer, so I turn and face him.

"So, what did you want to talk about Hunter?" I ask, keeping the island between us.

"I don't even know where to start," he says as he brushes a hand through his dark hair.

"How about I go first," I say and wish I could take it back. I didn't know where to start any more than he does. I take a breath, blowing it out to calm my nerves before I speak. "When I went to the hospital for the scan, I was with Cherry. She agreed to come with me in case you didn't make it. I had no doubts that you would be there though. I trusted what you felt for us," I rub my hand over my tummy, not sure if I was comforting my son or myself. "While we were there we got a call to say Frankie had been attacked and he was in bad shape, so I made Cherry leave and go to him. I was still waiting for you when Dean strode in. I was shocked to see him, but he explained that his friend's wife had just had a baby. In my worried and confused state I didn't question it too much." I look down as shame at my stupid naivety crowds me. I look up suddenly as I feel Hunter's hand on mine.

It gives me the courage to continue. "Anyway, Dean offered to stay with me until you came. I went to the toilet and when I returned I could have sworn I smelled your cologne, I even looked around for you. Dean confirmed you had been there and that you'd told him you had changed your mind and wanted me to either terminate the pregnancy or take the envelope that was filled with cash and leave you alone, that you wanted nothing to do with our son."

I look up to see a swirl of emotions in Hunter's eyes as I fight back my own emotions at reliving the heartbreak I had felt at hearing those words.

"I was devastated, I was so sure you were the one for me, the missing link in my heart."

"I am, Lexi. None of what he said was true," Hunter says as he stands and starts to move toward me.

I hold up a hand to stop him. "Please don't," I ask and see hurt cross his handsome face. Luckily, he accepts it and goes back to sitting opposite me.

"Afterwards, we went to the restaurant and saw you. You know what happened there. Dean lied to everyone and convinced me to let him stay here. I had no idea what he was capable of." A sob tears from my throat and I force it back down.

"Pretty Girl, please, you're killing me," he says as he stands and ignoring my outstretched hand this time, gathers me into his big, strong, safe arms. His scent, the feel of him, so familiar gives me the strength to carry on.

"I found out he had been cheating on me even before the stroke. When he realized I knew, he attacked me. I could hear you at the door, but he knocked me out. When I came to he was gone. I called Cherry and spent the next few days in the hospital. While I was in hospital Dean got back in and must have erased my emails as he has been doing all along. I found out and tried to contact you, but everything was shut down."

"I came to your office to try and see you and your friend told me you had gone to China with your fiancée." At these words I stiffen and pull away from his hold. He lets me go but doesn't move away.

"I'm so sorry, Lex. I was so hurt when I thought you had lied and I reacted badly. You have no idea how much I regret what happened. I did come to the hospital and I spoke with Dean, he told me the baby was his and you were mentally unstable and did this a lot." Hunter begins to pace as he speaks, and I try to fight the pain and betrayal I feel toward him for believing Dean over me.

"I don't know why I believed him over you. I was an idiot and I knew I'd made a mistake when I saw you at the restaurant. I have never met anyone as honest and loyal as you." He steps closer and reaches out his hand, fingering a blue strand of my hair. I close my eyes to savor the feeling of him close to me, knowing it might be the last time.

"I went home and sent you that email. When you didn't show I assumed the worst and like an idiot, I reacted very badly. I'm so sorry for that," his voice is husky as he speaks, and I believe him. Hunter is a good man— the problem is I can't trust him now and I'm not prepared to risk my heart or my baby for him or anyone again.

"I believe you," I say, and I feel a shudder go through his big frame as he leans his forehead against mine. I allow myself to enjoy it for a second before I step away.

"Can we start again, Lex?" he asks.

My wayward heart screamed yes, but she has got me into so much trouble that her voting rights have been revoked. My head is in charge now and she says no. I shake my head in the negative.

"I'm sorry, Hunter, I can't risk it. I know you are sorry and I know your feelings were genuine, the same as mine were, but you chose to believe a man you didn't know and saw the worst in me rather than trusting me. I can't risk it happening again."

"It wasn't all my fault, Lex. I accept my part in it but please don't punish me for what your ex has done. Yes, I should have trusted you, but you could have believed in me too." His words hit their mark, I know what he says is true, but I can face my anger toward Hunter. What I feel toward Dean is just too complex, the humiliation and fury, and being duped for so long. But I also know that I'm pushing Hunter away because he has a power over me that

Dean never had. If Hunter ever betrays me I feel I will splinter into a million pieces if I let it out.

"You said *were*. My feeling for you haven't changed, Lex. I love you." He implores softly, and my heart almost shatters with pain. Tears prick my eyes and I let them fall.

"I will always love you, Hunter, but it doesn't matter, the trust is gone now. I won't stop you from seeing your son and being part of his life, but we can't be anything other than friends," I look down to try and stem the tide of emotions that are hitting me like a fucking tsunami. When I look up there are tears in Hunter's eyes as he moves closer.

"I will prove to you that I can be trusted, Lex. You're my blue haired Pretty Girl, and I won't let you go ever again. Even if it takes my whole life to prove to you how much I love you, I will do it. You are my heart. It only beats for you," he says as he tilts my chin up so our eyes meet. His touch burns through me, my entire body is tingling with need for him.

He lowers his head and I let him, needing to taste him one more time before I say goodbye. His kiss when it comes is bittersweet, it is soft, it is sensual, and it feels like the most beautiful, tender touch, almost like a promise. But promises could be broken and I won't survive the next time. He pulls away and I see so much in his face, I believe he cares for me and I know he will be an amazing father, but all I can offer him is friendship.

"Goodbye, Hunter," I whisper.

"See you soon, Pretty Girl," he says as he kisses my forehead.

CHAPTER SIX

HUNTER

I'D HARDLY SLEPT A WINK LAST NIGHT, TOSSING AND turning thinking about all that was said between us. Lexi had nearly broken me, what she's gone through, the bruises on her face. It makes me want to rip Dean to shreds. I've put a call into the detective handling her case first thing this morning and have an appointment to meet with him later. It is times like this that having more money than God helps.

My mother walks into the kitchen as I'm loading up on caffeine and stops short.

"You're up early, darling," she says as she kisses my cheek and looks at me as if she is evaluating my health. It is a look only mothers can do.

"Yes, I have a lot do before I go over to Lexi's." I told my mother the whole story last night when I returned from seeing her. I had been in pretty bad shape when I'd returned, shaken by the sight of her and hearing what she had suffered at the hands of a madman. Mom had been surprisingly supportive and offered some good advice.

"Let me make you some breakfast then, you can't go into battle on an empty stomach." She smiles, and I see again the beautiful woman she still is.

"Thanks, mom." I smile at her turn of phrase, she doesn't know how close she is about going into battle. This is probably the most important takeover of my life and I need to strategize how I'm going to convince the woman I love that I can be trusted.

"Corned beef hash or cinnamon buns?" she asks as she started taking out pans.

"Corned beef."

"Cinnamon buns," my father and I both call at the same time. My mother laughs as he kisses her cheek.

"How about I do both?" she laughs at us.

"Thanks, ma," I say as my phone rings—it's Jake again. Things have been strained between us since I found out how he treated Lexi. I need to grow up though. Walking away, I answer the call.

"Yes?"

"Oh, hey, Mac."

"What do you need Jake? I'm in a hurry," I say in a clipped tone, he is my best friend and while a part of me knows he's sorry and was only looking out for me the other part needs to show him that it was not okay. I hear a sigh on the other end of the call before he speaks again.

"When are you going to stop treating me like a leper?" he asks.

"When I know you've got the message, Jake."

"Fine, but to know that you need to speak to me, let me prove I'm sorry." I think about how I have to do the exact same thing with Lexi.

"Fine, I need you to make sure the finance director doesn't fuck this China deal. He is playing hardball and I need you to reign him in. You're the only one I trust to do it."

"You got it, Mac," he replies, I can hear the relief in his voice.

"Keep me posted and if you can't get hold of me, call dad."

"No problem. And, Mac?"

"Yes?"

"I really am sorry."

"I know man, now go kick ass and make me more money," I laugh as I hung up. Money has never meant a lot to me but maybe that was because I had money. Which makes me think about the trust fund I've set up for my son. *My son.* It still seems so surreal to think in a few short months I will be a father.

Going back into the kitchen I observe my parents for the first time as an equal, not seeing them as my parents but as two people who really loved each other. My mother made a huge mistake but as I watch them as they laugh and cook together I realize that we all make mistakes and there was no doubt of the love they shared now. I just wished—as I always did—that my father's blood actually ran through my veins.

CHAPTER SEVEN

HUNTER

Knocking on the door I wait impatiently for Lexi to answer, hearing her open the locks I smile, pleased that she had so many door locks. As she swings the door open, I'm struck again by how beautiful she is. Even bruised and pale she was the most beautiful woman I had ever seen with her hair waving down her back. She is wearing blue jeans and a pale yellow and violet-flowered top that accentuated her pregnant curves, and it makes my mouth water.

"Hunter!" she exclaims surprise written on her pretty face.

"Hi," I say as I sweep past her not giving her a chance to shut the door in my face.

She closes the door and spins to look at me. "What are you doing here?' she asks, her surprise at seeing me working to my advantage.

"I thought you might want some help. You said you wanted to get your garden sorted before the realtor brings anyone around. So, I came to help."

"Oh, well... I guess. But I can manage, it's only tidying up and I can get someone over to fix the paneling."

"No need, I can do it," I smile and walk through the back door before letting myself out. I knew if I gave Lexi time to think it would allow her to shore up her defenses against me and I wasn't letting that happen. I feel her behind me as I walk to the storage shed at the back of the garden.

I open it, taking out everything I need to do the jobs before I turn to Lexi. "Shall we go and grab the panels before we get started?"

She looks at me and blinks slowly as if she is catching up to the conversation. "Yes, let's do that," she says as a small smile creeps across her face before she smothers it. I grin inwardly, *baby steps was still progress*. I watch as Lexi locks up and puts the alarm on.

She starts to walk to her car, but I stop her. "Let's take mine, it's bigger."

She quirks an eyebrow at me as she looks at my truck before she walks past me muttering. "Yeah, I know it is," she says so low I almost don't catch it.

I grin at her smart mouth but keep quiet not wanting her to realize how much she's already relaxing. As we drive to the Green Garden supplies store I ask her about the shop and how things were doing. She tells me about some of the designs she has drawn and promises to show me if when I ask to see them.

Lexi is one hell of a designer and successful in her own right. I know I have no right to be, but I'm so damn proud of her. We get everything we need at the store and I load it into the back of my truck. She tries to lift some plants and I nearly lose my mind.

"Lexi," I growl with a frown as I take them from her.

"Hunter," she mimics back in the same tone.

"You shouldn't be lifting anything."

"I'm not helpless," she says as she crosses her arms over her chest, pushing her beautiful tits up. My eyes drop, my balls tighten. God, I needed to be inside her again, but I can't rush this, I need to make her feel safe, feel loved.

"Hunter," she shouts, and my eyes jump to her face where she is smirking at me. I had been caught red-handed.

"Sorry, but you are so fucking beautiful." A blush creeps over her neck and up her face at my words and I growl. "Lexi do not look at me like that."

"Like what?" she asks all innocence.

"You know what," I say as I cross to take the plants from beside her legs. I watch as she walks away and groan inwardly. I need to fix this, and soon.

We spend the afternoon getting the garden fixed, with me doing all the heavy work, like changing fence panels and mowing. Lexi plants some borders and tubs in the front. When we are done, it's early afternoon. I walk closer to her as she puts away her gardening gloves and shears.

"Want to grab a late lunch?' I ask casually. I see from the look on her face that she wants to but she's holding back.

"I don't think it's a good idea," she responds slowly.

"It's only lunch, Lex. We both have to eat, right?"

I see uncertainty cross her pretty face before she gives in. "Fine but I'm buying."

"Yes, Ma'am," I reply with a crooked grin, knowing there is no way she is paying.

We grab a late lunch at Wendy's and chat about safe

topics like movies, art, and work before it inevitably comes around to Lola.

"So, what happened with your fiancée?" Lexi asks as she stirs sugar into her decaf coffee. I try to quell the desire to pump my fist in the air at the jealous tone of her voice. Lexi is practically green with jealousy which means she still cares.

"I've known Lola for years. We dated on and off, but it was never serious for me. When I ran away to China, I took her with me as a rebound reaction to a hurt I mistakenly blamed you for."

"I see." Lexi lowers her head, so I can't see her eyes.

"Lexi look at me," I call as I reach across the table to lift her chin to meet my eyes. They are bright with unshed tears and swimming with the pain I had put there. I had thought that my regret had reached its limit but every time I see the pain I've put there I feel worse.

"I know I hurt you, Pretty Girl, but I never touched Lola. She tried to get me to notice her but all I could think about was you. As soon as we landed I knew I had made a mistake." I get up and crouch down beside her chair, taking her hands in mine. "All I could think about was you. I didn't even care that the baby might not be mine. It was always you I wanted, I haven't looked at another woman since we spent the best night of my life together."

I feel a tear hit my hand and I thumb away the ones that run silently down her cheeks. The pain hits me square in the chest, twisting my gut to know what I did to the woman I loved. "I'm so sorry. I promise you, Lexi, if it takes a lifetime to do it I will prove how much I love you. Give me a chance to show you."

Her hand comes out to stroke my cheek and I close my eyes at the feel of her hands on me. "I love you too,

Hunter, but I'm so scared. I don't think I could take losing you again. It hurt too much."

"You won't lose me, Pretty Girl. I'm in this until the end," I whisper as I lift her into my arms.

"Give me some time," she asks.

I feel hope bloom in my chest. "Okay, Lex. I can do that. Now, how about we get out of here?"

"Okay." She grins then, and it's the first genuine smile I've seen from her in months. It makes my heart sing and a weight lifts from my shoulders.

CHAPTER EIGHT

LEXI

"Everything looks great, Lexi. You are exactly where you need to be for twenty-seven weeks," Dr O'Connor says as he hands me some tissues to wipe the ultrasound gel from my tummy. I take a grinning Hunter's hand as he pulls me to a sitting position and return his smile.

This feeling right now is the one I had been missing the last few times I had been to the doctor's office—contentment, euphoria, love for my baby, for the man beside me.

Even though I'm still holding Hunter at a distance, things between us have shifted. We've settled into a pattern over the last six and half weeks where Hunter spends every day with me, no matter what we are doing. The only times he's left me is when I was at the shop with Cherry.

He hasn't spent the night with me yet, but he's spent a few on my sofa.

"Thank you, Lexi," he says as I stand, pulling my clothes straight. Hunter kisses my forehead tenderly and for just a second, I close my eyes and let all the other worries disappear.

"You did half the work, Hunter," I say then laugh.

He takes my hand as we follow Dr O'Connor into his office. We take a seat, side by side, my hand still in Hunters as we wait for the doctor to come in and give me the all-clear.

His leg bounces beside me as we wait, so I put a hand out to steady him. It stops instantly, and he looks at me. "Sorry, I'm nervous. I know little man is okay, but I just want to make sure you are." He smiles self-consciously.

God, could I love this man more? The answer was no, but even now I'm scared that he will get cold feet.

I'd discussed it with Cherry, Frankie, and Darla and they have all agreed I should go for it. They've settled nicely into 'team Hunter'—the traitors.

"I feel fine Hunter." I try to reassure him but since everything that had gone on, he is ultra-protective. The door opens, and Dr O'Connor walks in with some papers. His face is impassive as he sits down behind his desk.

He looks up and smiles and I feel relief hit my stomach. After everything that has happened, it has been niggling at the back of my head that something might be wrong.

"Well, as I said before, Lexi, the baby is growing well. He measures in the seventy-fifth percentile, so he is looking to be a big boy." He casts a look at Hunter and smiles. "I'm guessing that's from his father though."

I looked at Hunter with a smile and squeeze his hand as he grins back.

"Yes, I was a big baby. Made my sweet, southern mama cuss like a sailor. Or so I'm told—often." He laughs as does Dr O'Connor.

"Well, we will monitor Lexi closely over the next thirteen weeks, so she should be fine."

Hunter and I leave the doctor's office, my hand tucked in his, a feeling of complete contentment in my heart.

Hunter helps me into the car and before seating himself in the driver's seat, he turns to me before we drive off. "Thank you, Lexi, for letting me be a part of this, for giving me the chance to show you the man I can be." His words make my throat clog, he thinks I have given him a gift, but I'm the lucky one and day by day he is chipping away at the walls I have built to protect myself.

"You're very welcome Hunter," I say softly.

We are on our way to meet his parents for lunch. It was my idea. My son would need good people in his life and as my parents spend so much time out of the country now, I want him to be close to his other grandparents. Hunter is overjoyed with my suggestion but has seen the nerves kicking in so suggested we meet at a neutral place for lunch.

As we pull up at the National Exemplar, I feel a frisson of nerves in my belly. I take a calming breath and look up as Hunter takes my hand.

"Relax, Lex. My mom is going to love you and my dad already does," he says with a reassuring smile. His blue eyes are twinkling as he helps me from the car. I hold tight to my bag as we cross the parking lot, determined not to give them the wrong impression as I keep my hands busy. Things are not resolved with Hunter yet, and I don't want them thinking I'm leading him on.

Hunter has no such thoughts and when I won't give him my hand, he wraps his arm around what used to be my waist. He pulls me into his side and leans in close to my ear. "Stop worrying or you're going to make yourself sick." He kisses my cheek as he pulls open the door for me to go ahead of him.

"I can if want to," I say as I poke my tongue out at him. He laughs and then looks up and to the side of me.

"Mom, Dad," he says with a grin. I close my eyes knowing that they had both just seen me poke my tongue out at their son like a two-year-old child and want the floor to open underneath me. Plastering a smile on my face, I turn to face Hunter's parents.

They are both looking at me with smiles on their faces.

"Any chance you didn't see that?" I ask with a hopeful smile. Hank laughs and reaches forward, kissing both my cheeks. He grasps my arms and looks me over in a discerning, parental way.

"My dear girl, you look like a picture," he says with a kind smile.

"Thank you, Hank," I reply as I catch Hunter's mother watching us quietly. *Please let her be nice.* She is a strikingly beautiful woman, who looks way younger than the fifty-six that Hunter said she is. I thought she would take my hand but as her husband had done she leans in and kisses my cheeks.

"It's a pleasure to meet you, Lexi," she says in the most beautiful southern drawl.

"You too, Ma'am," I reply not knowing what I should call her. For some reason, she scares me more than Hank does. Maybe it's because I'm starting to see it from a mother's point of view. I can't imagine how I might react if this was my son.

"Please call me Vivian, all my friends do. I have a feeling we are going to be friends." she smiles as she hooks her arm through mine and leads us toward our table.

Lunch has been surprisingly relaxed, Hunter keeps close to my side, offering silent support as I chat with his mom and dad. They were to my relief both lovely people. I can't help making the comparison between them and Dean's parents, who had practically disappeared from our lives once we were married, only exchanging cards and the odd holiday visit. Which was nothing like today, they had always seemed so buttoned up and strained as if they couldn't wait to be away from us.

"Have you thought of any names yet?" Vivian asks as we eat a dessert of lemon tart and vanilla cream. I look at Hunter and he looks at me.

"No, not yet. Things have been a little crazy, so I haven't thought about it."

"And what about a surname? Will the baby be a McKenzie?" she asks with a sugary sweetness that did not fool me for a second.

"Ma!"

"Vivian!"

Hank and Hunter both exclaim at the same time, making me laugh.

"Well played, Vivian," I say as both men watch us, looking slightly nervous.

"What? I like her. I don't want her to get away," she says in a hushed tone to Hank as Hunter drops his head to my shoulder.

"Kill me now," he murmurs but I can tell he isn't angry with her, not really. I pat his cheek lovingly as I kiss his head.

"Poor baby." His hand slips behind me as the other grazes my bump.

"Just for the record, McKenzie gets my vote," he whispers. His sexy blue eyes bore into me, as I hold his gaze. He is so handsome, but more than that. He is kind, generous, funny, attentive, and he lets me be me. I love this man and it is getting harder and harder to remember why I'm keeping him at arm's length.

"I tell you what, you pick his first name and I'll decide on the second name. How does that sound?"

"That sounds like a promise," he says as he kisses me hard. Noise falls away as he kisses me with a tenderness I can't remember feeling before, not from anyone. A clearing of throats brings us back to the present as we break apart and look at his smiling parents.

"See Hank, a mother knows best," Vivian says with a smug grin as Hank pays the bill and we walk out into the spring sunshine with me tucked into Hunters side, secure in his arms. We are walking across the parking lot when my cell rings. Routing through my bag I find my phone and answer it. It is the realtor.

"Mrs. Crane, It's Phil Donaldson from Move4You. The people who viewed the house yesterday have put in an offer they would like you to consider."

"Okay, what is it?"

He tells me the figure which is thirty thousand less than the asking price. No way was I taking that, I had already dropped the price for a quick sale.

"No way. It's a bargain at the asking price we listed it at. Tell them to up their offer," I reply as Hunter watches me, a question in his eyes as we stand beside the car.

"Really, Mrs. Crane, you should consider this offer. A

little lady in your predicament should be grateful for any offers at all."

I pull the phone away from my ear and look at it trying to figure out if he was serious or if he had lost his Goddamned mind.

"You're so right, Mr. Donaldson. I'm on my way to your offices to discuss it now." I purr sweetly as my blood boils with rage.

"That is a very wise move, Ma'am." I can't listen to his weaselly voice for one more second, so I disconnect the call. In a fit of rage, I hurl the phone at the wall and scream. *That no good, low life piece of pond scum.* How *dare* he treat me like that.

"Lex?" Hunter asks as he approaches me slowly, a worried look on his face. "At the risk of getting punched, calm down and tell me who that was and what they said."

I look at the worried faces of Hunter, Hank, and Vivian and try to get my anger under control.

"I'm sorry. I'm fine, really. I just need to take care of some things at the realtor's office."

"What did he say?" Hank asks as he and Vivian moved in beside Hunter.

I relay the conversation and watch as Hunter's eyes darken with anger.

"That bastard! Well, my instinct is to go over there and teach him some manners, but this is your call, Lexi. How do you want to handle this?"

I look at him, and for a second I'm shocked. *Is he asking me?* My entire marriage Dean had made me sit back and be the dutiful wife.

"I'm not sure but I won't do business with someone who can so easily treat me that way because I'm a woman."

"My dear, if you don't mind I have an idea," Vivian says. Her kind eyes twinkle with merriment and mischief.

"You don't need to get involved, Vivian. I'm sure you have loads to do and I don't want to take up any more of your time."

"Nonsense, this will be fun. Hunter, we will follow you two to the realtor's office. You let me handle this."

CHAPTER NINE

LEXI

I watch as Vivian waltzes into the realtor's office like she owns the place, her head high in exaggerated haughtiness that wasn't there before. I walk slowly behind her beside Hunter as Hank stands with his hand gently on the small of her back. He is letting her lead this but also letting anyone who is paying any attention know that she's speaking for them both and he has her back.

A young woman with mousy hair, and tortoiseshell glasses is sitting behind the reception desk. She looks up with a smile as we enter. "Hello, may I help you?" she asks.

"Yes, my dear. I would like to speak with Phillip Donaldson please," Vivian says with a smile.

"Let me just check if he is available." She picks up the phone and dials a number. I can see through to the offices at the back that he is there.

"Mr. Donaldson, I have someone here to speak with you." I can't hear what is being said on the other end, but the girl starts to go red, and looks flustered as we all hear him yelling at her. She hangs up and I see she is fighting back the tears. "I'm afraid Mr. Donaldson is busy and can't see anyone," she says.

I smile at her with sympathy knowing what an ass he is.

"Don't worry, my dear," Vivian says as she takes out her phone and dials. We all watch with bated breath. "Penelope, its Vivi. I'm terribly sorry to bother you but I have a small issue." She begins to explain what has happened to me and how Mr. Donaldson has treated me and then the way he has behaved toward the receptionist I turn to Hunter who is looking amused. He slips his hand into mine and squeezes.

Vivian hangs up with a smile. "Penelope is on her way."

I look to Hunter for meaning and he leans in to whisper in my ear, the softness of his lips tickling my ear. "Penelope owns this realty along with a few others. She and mom play bridge together every week." I gasp and slap my hand over my mouth to keep from laughing. "Do you want to look around?" he asks, and I nod my head. I need to find a house but have been putting it off.

I wander aimlessly as I'm looking at the properties just waiting for the right person to buy them and turn them into homes. Every one of these people will have a dream, a plan of how they want to see their future go, but the sad reality is that life very rarely deals you the hand you expect.

The door behind us opens and a tall, willowy blonde walks in. She epitomizes class, from her Chanel bag to her Prada heels. She says a few words to the girl at the reception who looks terrified, before she replies. Penelope seems to straighten her shoulders before lifting the receiver, dialing the number.

Over the line, I can hear Phillip Donaldson raging at what he thinks is the receptionist.

"Mr. Donaldson, if you have quite finished," she says in a sharp tone that brooks no argument. In seconds Mr. Donaldson is running through from his office straightening his tie.

"Mrs. Chiswell, what a lovely surprise," he says as he glances around at us all.

"Is it? Because from what I just heard, it's not pleasant."

"I apologize but the girl has been very lacking, she didn't bother to tell me these nice people were here," he says with a sneer as he attempts to save himself.

"Really? Because that's not what I heard."

"Well, I don't know what you heard but that's what happened."

I feel Hunter move behind me as Mr. Donaldson glares at me.

"Are you calling one of my oldest friends a liar, Mr. Donaldson?" she asks, and I can see sweat breaking out on his forehead. I'm not malicious but I'm enjoying this.

"What happened, Mandy?" Penelope asks the terrified receptionist.

Mandy relays what happened as Phillip Donaldson goes a funny puce color.

"That sounds like gross misconduct to me. Please gather your things and leave the premises immediately, Mr. Donaldson. Your services are no longer required."

With an angry glare and words of retribution, he storms from the room before gathering his things and pushing past Hunter and I as he leaves.

"I'm very sorry for this, Mrs. Crane. I can assure you

that we do not take kindly to the kind of sexist behavior you just witnessed."

"That's okay. Can you pass the message on to the people who offered way below the asking price for my house, that it was not accepted."

"It was him," Mandy speaks up then. We all look in her direction. "I mean, he and a friend have been buying up houses cheap and then selling them privately for the asking price."

"I believe we have some business to discuss, Mandy," Penelope says. She then kisses Vivian and Hank before moving to Hunter.

"Young man, you must come and see me soon. Simon would love to see you."

"I will, Penelope," Hunter replies as he allows her to pull him in for a hug.

We leave Hank and Vivian with a promise to see them soon. Today has been a good day. I haven't thought about Dean or the threat he poses to me once.

CHAPTER TEN

LEXI

"I CAN'T BELIEVE YOU'VE NEVER WATCHED STORAGE Wars," I say as I lie with my feet in Hunters lap.

"I can't believe you made me watch four episodes back to back," he says with a smirk. He takes my feet in his hands and starts to massage the base. His hands are strong and sure, and I practically groan in contentment. It's been two weeks since our lunch with Vivian and Hank. I've since met Cassie, Hunters sister and her daughter Mellie who is completely adorable.

Watching Hunter with Mellie made my toes curl with happiness. He is going to be an amazing father. I feel Hunter's firm hands as he massages my legs and I sink further into the couch as my body turns liquid. His hand moves higher and higher, lightly caressing the inside of my leg.

Warmth spreads from his hands to every erogenous zone I have. I feel like heat and desire is licking me all over. We have kissed but nothing else. Part of me is worried that he doesn't find me attractive anymore, but if the hardness under my leg is anything to go by then maybe I'm wrong.

His large body looms over me, his lips inches from mine. We watch each other, the play of emotions casting a spell on us. We are in a bubble where only the two of us exist, his blue eyes are dark, almost indigo with need. A fire licks up my side where he touches me with a feather-light touch. It is not meant to be arousing, it's as if he can't help touching me.

"I need to be with you, Pretty Girl," he whispers, his voice husky.

I don't answer but I move so that he is cradled between my thighs. He holds his weight off me with his arm on the couch beside my shoulder. The heat of his hard cock presses against my core and I try and suppress the urge to move against him and taking what I need from him.

His lips are soft as he flicks his tongue against my lips seeking entrance. Our tongues tangle as we kiss, igniting the flames of our desire for one another. Our breath is coming in harsh gasps as he tears his mouth away.

"Is this what you want, Lex?" he asks, and I can tell he's holding on to his control by a thread. His jaw clenches, his muscles are shaking.

"Yes," I breathe. I want this. I'm sick of fighting what I know is my destiny. Since the second our eyes locked across the bar, we have been destined for this. He is the missing piece in the puzzle, the calm to my storm. We hurt each other, yes, but we are also the only ones who can fix the ache in other's heart.

Hunter stands and in one swift movement I'm in his arms, cradled against his chest and the safety it offers me.

Hunter carries me upstairs, placing me on my bed. We don't speak, not needing words. Both of us know what this is, we know that everything is changing, coming together as it should have been from the start.

I watch from the bed as he unbuttons his shirt, exposing the hard-muscled chest that leads down to a defined six-pack. The dark smattering of hair that tapers down to the ridged V of muscle makes me pant. I have no more time to think as he comes toward me, a predator about to claim his prey.

I'm his prey, but I'm also his gift and the reverence with which he treats me makes me want to weep. I feel cherished and loved, like a tiny Dresden doll that will break if handled too harshly. Hunter falls to his knees in front of me pulling me to the edge of the bed by the backs of my knees.

I feel my core clench with the need to be filled by him, claimed by this man who has stolen my heart and given me back my soul. His hands travel over me as he unbuttons my shirt, kissing my neck before following it with his tongue down to the curve of my breasts that are held barely in place by the lace cups.

"I've had some very impure thoughts about these breasts," he says with a wolfish grin.

"Yeah?"

"Yeah," he replies.

"Show me," I rasp.

Hunter needs no further encouragement. He swoops his mouth to the round fullness of my tender breasts, unhooking the clasp and letting them spill free.

"Magnificent." He looks like a starving man as he takes me in his mouth, sucking gently on the peak. It feels as if there is a direct line from my nipple to my clit as he sucks, eliciting a moan from me. I rock my hips against him as he administers the same sweet torture to the other breast.

I feel his hand smooth over the rounded curve of my tummy, his eyes wide in awe.

"You're so beautiful like this. I think we should keep you pregnant with my child forever." His words unlock a wantonness in me, making me feel desirable and beautiful as only Hunter can.

"I need you inside me, Hunter," I moan as his hand slips into the waistband of my leggings, pushing them down my legs. Next to go are my panties. I'm now fully exposed to him. I move to close my legs, embarrassed by how wet and how unkempt I probably am.

His hand stops me, and he looks at me sharply. "Are you mine, Lexi?" he asks.

I know it has more meaning than I can fathom right now but I don't hesitate to answer. "Yes. I'm yours."

"And I'm yours. Don't hide what is mine from me," he says as he eases my legs apart.

I feel open and exposed as his eyes wander over my pussy. Heat settles in me like a live electric current. I'm strong, I know that with my submission I'm bringing this powerful man to his knees.

I hold all the power as I let myself succumb to his gaze.

"Fucking beautiful," he murmurs as his mouth moves over my clit. My body arches off the bed as he sucks and licks until I'm a liquid pool of need. My body is a desperate quivering mass of nerve endings as he plays me like I'm the sweetest of symphonies. My climax peeks and I feel myself on the precipice waiting to fall, just waiting for something.

"Come for me, love," he says as he thrusts two fingers inside me, curling until he hits that sweet spot that makes my vision haze over with a rainbow of color. My world shifts as the orgasm is ripped from me.

I feel Hunter kiss his way over my tummy toward my lips. I taste myself on him and it's erotic and forbidden. I'm ruined for anyone but this man, and I see from his expression that he knows it too.

With a swift motion, Hunter is up and shedding his clothes. I watch in a glazed haze of need as he strips, then he's standing in front of me, his cock hard, proud in his nakedness. I wonder how this will work, but Hunter has no such issues. He moves to grab a condom and I stay his hand.

"I'm clean, the hospital tests these things," I say with a hint of a blush touching my cheeks.

"I am, too. I'm tested every few months, but I have never gone bare before, not with anyone," he says.

I know we used a condom, but I guess it is one more way of showing we are destined.

I hold my arms to him and he slips behind me, turning me to my side. His body fits mine and I feel his hardness in the cheeks of my ass. He moves against me as he cups my breasts in his hands, pinching the nipples softly. I moan and arch my back, pushing into his hand.

"Hunter please."

Lifting my top leg, he angles it back over his thigh as he pushes his cock through the wetness of my lips, coating it with my need. Kisses along my neck make me tilt my head to give him full access to my body.

Pushing forward he enters me and at once I feel the missed fullness of him, a groan in my ear tells me he feels how good it is too. Rocking back, he pulls out before seating himself again.

"Fuck. You feel so good. Nothing. Fucking. Better," he

groans as he begins to rock into me, finding a rhythm that quickly becomes desperate. My climax is building as he rubs my clit in circles, faster and faster, matching the speed of his hips as he slams into me. His name is torn from my throat as I climax hard, clamping down on his length.

"Fuck me, Lexi," he moans as I feel his warm seed spill into me, coating me, and branding me as his. We are both breathing hard by the time I collapse onto his arm.

He turns my head and our eyes catch and we both know that everything has changed now. We started as two and now we are one, our connection cemented in the love we share.

Hunter moves, and I hiss at the loss of him, but he is soon back with a cloth to wipe away the evidence of our lovemaking. I feel his heat at my back as he climbs back into bed and cradles my back to his front. I can't remember ever feeling like this—he is my savior and my strength, and I'm his.

"I love you so much, Pretty Girl."

"I love you too Hunter," I whisper.

There is nothing that can touch us now.

CHAPTER ELEVEN

LEXI

I WAKE WITH A START— MY HEART IS RACING AS THE fragments of nightmare float through my foggy brain. I grasp at fragmented images as they play out in a reel just out of reach. I lie in Hunter's arms as he snores softly behind me, his hard chest offering protection like a cocoon.

I hear rain on the windows, it is heavy but instead of the normal comfort I feel from the sound it makes me shiver. The clock on the nightstand reads 02:47. I snuggle under the covers as I try and go back to sleep, but the nightmare is plaguing me—the fact that I can't remember what it was about doesn't seem to matter, my psyche remembers even if I don't.

Giving up I decide to go and get a glass of water to try and clear my mind. Gently I slip out from beneath Hunter's arm and snag the nightshirt that is at the end of the bed. Padding downstairs, I make my way to the kitchen. I take a glass from the cupboard and open the fridge to pour myself a drink.

As I do, the light from the fridge catches on the French windows that lead out to my garden. I turn in almost slow motion, my heart rate accelerating, my throat clogged with fear as I see a woman with her face pressed to the glass. She is soaking wet, her hair hanging in ratty ropes down her face, black streaks of mascara running down her face.

The thin white dress is plastered to her skin as she looks at me. She looks like a broken china doll, thin and pale. Her eyes are wild and yet dead at the same time as she stares at me with one hand on the glass. I don't know how long I stare back but it's only seconds before a scream tears from my throat as I see the blood dripping from her wrists, the knife hanging loosely in the hand at her side.

I closed the fridge and turn to flee the terrifying scene. I run headlong into a hard chest as hands grip me tight around my shoulders and I fight, pushing away from the grip until my mind can filter the noise and feel of Hunter. I sag into his arms as my entire body shakes from the fear running through my blood.

"Lexi, Pretty Girl, talk to me. What is it?" he says as he cradles me in his arms, safe, always safe, when he is around me. I haul in a lungful of air as I try and calm myself long enough to explain to him.

"A woman, she has a knife," I whisper, my voice hoarse from screaming.

I feel his body stiffen, ready for a fight as he backs me away from the window where I'm pointing. "Lexi go to the bedroom and call the police. Lock the door until I come find you," he murmurs pulling away.

My entire body freezes at the thought of being alone,

even for a second but I know it's the right thing. I nod my head as I force my heavy, cold feet to move.

Closing the door, I turn the lock and move to sit on the bed as coldness invades my body, my fingers are shaking as I dial 911 on my cell.

"Police, what is your emergency?"

"There's a woman at my back door, she..." I stutter over the words before taking a deep breath. "She has a knife,"

"Is anyone hurt, Ma'am?"

"I'm not sure, she has blood on her arms, but it's dark and I couldn't see." I'm shaking with cold.

"We have officers on route to you now, Ma'am. Is there anyone else in the house with you?"

"Yes, my boyfriend is downstairs."

"Okay. Stay on the line with me until you hear the officers at your door."

As I listen for any slight sound, worry for Hunter plagues me as I keep seeing the woman in my mind's eye. I jump a foot when Hunter knocks on the bedroom door.

"Lex, it's me."

I move quickly, opening the door to him. He immediately takes me in his arms and cradles me to his side as he moves us to the bed. Gently he extracts the phone from my hand and puts it to his ear.

It is only then that I notice he's only wearing jeans, his top and feet are bare—even the buttons of his jeans are open.

As Hunter is moving us downstairs, the police start banging on the door. We sit on the couch as the two officers do a sweep of the property outside.

Hunter hasn't left my side and I can't imagine going through this alone tonight. I barely notice the blanket that is around my shoulders as I shiver. Only the sound of his heartbeat is keeping me grounded, and his warm scent surrounds me. I have relinquished control of the situation to him not wanting to deal with anyone right now. I guess I trust him a more than I thought possible.

"Lex." His voice calls me, and I look up to see the investigating officer from my case with Dean standing before me.

"Sorry, yes?" I ask as he looks at me with pity.

He bends down on his haunches so that we are at eye level. "Mr. McKenzie has his surveillance guys sending the file from this evening up until we arrived on scene. If there was anyone out there it will show on the CCTV footage."

"Don't you believe me?" I say, my voice sharp with indignation.

"Of course, we do, but we still need to see the footage to check what you saw or rather who. We can't discount the fact that Dean Crane is still at large."

I feel the familiar curl of fear and fury wind through me at the name of my soon to be ex-husband, but under-neath all of that is shame. Shame that I did not see him for what he was.

"Mr. McKenzie, will you be staying with Mrs. Crane?"

I feel the arm around me go tense at the name and I understand it, because every time I hear it, it feels like nails are being dragged along a chalkboard.

"Lexi will be coming to stay with me until he is caught, along with the woman she saw," he says hotly, and I let my shoulders sag at his words—he believes me. I know I should fight him for being so domineering and bossy, not consulting or asking me about leaving this house. But as I look around I don't feel a warmth that I used to feel. I feel fear, like the walls are watching me, as if every time I walk into a room I will see Dean waiting for me, to finish what he started.

"Very good. Well we will contact you as soon as we hear anything," Detective Walker stands and moves toward the officer who is waiting to speak with him.

"How are you holding up?" Hunter asks as he lifts my chin, so he can look into my eyes.

I nod. "Okay I guess. I just can't get the image out of my head. I just want all this to be over."

"It will be, Pretty Girl. I'm going to get someone private on it, you shouldn't have to deal with this. We'll catch Dean and whoever you saw tonight and get you safe again. I promise. Would you like to stay at my Condo or would you prefer to stay at my parent's house?"

"Can we stay at your condo tonight? I don't want to drag anyone else into this."

Hunter kisses my head. "Of course. Let's get you dressed and I'll pack a bag for you. He won't get to you, Lex. I promise I'll free you from this monster,"

I know Hunter means it, but as a cold chill sweeps down my neck a feeling of foreboding hits me, making me turn to look out at the black nothingness behind me. I wonder what the cost of my freedom will be?

CHAPTER TWELVE

HUNTER

POURING THE THOUSAND-DOLLAR BRANDY INTO A crystal decanter, I fight to control fury that pulses through me. Lexi is finally asleep in my bed, calm and safe in the luxury penthouse I own. I slump down onto the black leather couch, my mind and body buzzing with the primal need to fight, to fix the situation.

The scream from Lex is still ringing in my ears, her fear is etched in my brain. I had been on my way to find her when I heard the scream that was ripped from her throat. Running my hand over my tired eyes I think back to the conversation we'd had with the detective handling this case and feel my anger rise anew.

He believes Dean is gone, the case is on the back burner for him. I'm not convinced he even believed Lexi, but he didn't see the very real fear on her face or feel the way she clung to me, her heart racing. When I asked what they were doing to find Dean they told me all the normal bullshit.

They were making inquiries, talking to people, following leads. But it's not enough. He is out there. I can feel it, and now she does too. She's tried to hide it from me, but I see her, the real Lexi. She's scared, and it isn't good for her or our son. And it's not acceptable, she deserves to be able to enjoy this time in her life and damn it so do I.

With that thought in my head, I come to a decision. What is the point of being richer than God if you can't use it when you need it? Grabbing my phone off the glass coffee table, I scroll the contacts pausing as I come to my PI's number, before dismissing him. This job is bigger than him. I want this dealt with in a permanent manner.

I know Lexi may hate me for it, but I will not let her feel paralyzing fear when I'm able to do something about it. I protect what is mine and Lexi is mine. I hit call and let the number ring out.

"Speak."

"It's me, I have a job for you."

"What kind of job?"

"The type that needs a secure line!"

"This line is always secure."

"I need somebody found and when they are found I need them gone. For good."

A pause on the line is brief as he processes what I'm saying. "How soon?"

"Immediately," I respond knowing that I'm potentially passing a point that I can't return from.

"Send me all the details in the usual manner," he says in his clear British accent.

"Thank you," I say as a sense of calmness comes over me.

"I'll be in touch." The line goes dead.

For the first time since I saw Lexi and the bruises that covered her beautiful face, I feel like things are swinging in our favor.

Tipping back the brandy in one motion—the smooth burn relaxes me—before I stand and move through my penthouse to double check the security system is set. The smooth tile flooring is warm on my bare feet from the underfloor heating. I check the doors to the balcony before I move on to the security panel. This security system is better than the top of the range, it's custom built.

The good thing about having money and friends in high places is you can have the best gadgets in the world, and right now I have never been happier with my need for security. The panel is blinking to show all zones of the penthouse are secure. The panic room is stocked, I have my top people looking through the CCTV from Lexi's place, and the deadliest person I know is now on the hunt for Dean.

There is nothing more I can do except wait and the only place I want to do that is curled up next to Lexi. I make my way back to my room and stand at the door, my shoulder leaning against the jam as I watch her sleep.

She is curled in a ball in the middle of the bed, her hands tucked under her cheek prayer style, her hair splayed out on the pillow around her, face relaxed in rest. She awes me every day with her strength, passion for life and the caring way she is with people. Nothing and nobody is ever forgotten once they are on her radar.

From the old guy that delivers her mail to the lady at the bank whose mother has had a hip operation. She remembers and makes people feel special. She makes me feel like I hung the moon for her, but she is still fiercely strong and independent.

I can't stand being far from her, even when I'm working I find myself thinking of her, wanting to speak to her, to see her smile, feel the gentle familiar touches as she goes about her business not knowing how she affects me.

I slip into bed behind her, pulling her gently to me. Her head settles in the crook of my shoulder and her warm breath is on my chest. I look at the ceiling of my bedroom as the dawn starts to filter through the blinds, the woman I love plastered to my side, her leg thrown over me and vow to myself that I will do whatever it takes to protect her.

CHAPTER THIRTEEN

LEXI

I WAKE TO THE SOUND OF HUNTER'S VOICE, I FEEL FUZZY headed and confused as I see the pale gray curtains that cover floor to ceiling windows. I'm disorientated as I slowly sit up, pushing my hair back from my face. Then I remember the woman at the window. A shiver goes through me and a memory of the fear I felt prickles my neck.

Thankfully my son decides it's time to play trampoline on my bladder and the need to go to the bathroom distracts me from my fear. I look around and spy what I remember is the bathroom, padding that way I take a good look around the bathroom that is the size of my living room.

The large jacuzzi bath, a double shower with multiple heads, sleek black tiles on the floor and chrome fixtures make the space feel stylish. Pure white towels are folded on the heated towel rail, a large wall length mirror is above the sink. I relieve my poor bladder and then decide to take a shower.

I strip Hunter's t-shirt that he gave me to sleep in and step into the warm steam of the hot shower. The heat hits my skin, the jets soothe the ache in my neck. I use the shower gel on the shelf to wash away the dirt and grime, letting the fear go from my muscles. The shower gel smells like Hunter and I like the feeling of him surrounding me. I could happily stay in here all day, not letting the outside world intrude but I know I have people who will need to know about last night—namely Cherry.

I step out wrapping myself in a fluffy white towel. Walking into the bedroom I see my bag on the bed and smile knowing Hunter put it there for me. He is always there when I need him—he won't even let me lift my handbag half the time. I should find it overbearing but I don't. I find it endearing. I know the fact that he didn't protect me from Dean is the cause. Hunter is a typical alpha male and not protecting what is his is unacceptable to him.

I dress quickly in maternity skinny jeans and white shirt before slipping my feet into pumps. I leave my hair damp, just throwing it into a ponytail before I move toward the sound of Hunter's voice. I stop to watch him as I come into the living space. He is leaning against the large kitchen island, his feet spread as he talks on his phone.

His handsome face is frowning, his jaw tense as he listens intently. He must sense me because he looks up. Our eyes lock, and a shiver runs through me at the intensity in them. His arm comes up as he stands away from the island. I slip beneath the curve of his shoulder, my front against his side as his arm wraps around me like a steel band. It feels good, safe, protected.

"Send me the files and don't tell anyone about this. I want the utmost discretion," Hunter says and from the tone of his voice, I shiver. This is a side of Hunter I have not seen. It is him at work, in control, the CEO of a multi-billion-dollar business. It's sexy as hell and as I stand there it hits me just how rich he is and just how different we are.

His suits probably cost more than my car, his penthouse has touches of luxury that are so understated that you know they must cost the earth. Something about the understated elegance hints at money, rather than the glaring garish adornments that scream money, tell the story of who he is more than anything.

He takes the phone from his ear after hanging up and kisses me lightly on the mouth. It is light, but my body responds anyway. Heat floods me so I open my mouth inviting him to deepen the kiss. He answers my unspoken invitation kissing me deeper, his tongue dancing with mine. He pulls away and we are both breathing hard even as he smiles.

"That's quite the good morning." He is smiling but the lines at his eyes show the worry he's trying to hide.

"I missed you," I say instead, not ready to let reality intrude for a few more seconds.

"You smell good," he says as he sniffs my neck.

"I used your shower gel."

"It smells better on you," he says as he kisses my neck before pulling away and turning toward the kitchen cupboards.

"That's a matter of opinion," I mutter as I watch him opening and closing cupboards as he pulls out a pan, eggs, bacon, and pancake mix.

"Hungry?" he asks as he holds up the eggs.

"Your son is always hungry." I laugh as my belly lets out

a growl.

"Let's get you fed then."

As he fries bacon in one pan, I flip pancakes in the one beside him. It feels like we have been doing this forever when in fact, we are so new to this.

Once breakfast is over and I'm full of delicious pancakes and bacon, I help him clear away the dishes. I know I can't avoid it any longer.

"Did we hear from the police yet?"

"No." He eyes me cautiously and I can tell there is more. For a second, I wonder if I even want to know but then remember that I'm strong and can deal with this.

"And?" I ask as I move closer, laying my hands on his chest, not sure if I'm offering comfort with my touch or taking it.

His arms come around me, holding me close as he looks at me. "My people have the CCTV and we have managed to identify the woman,"

I suck in a sharp breath as I process this news. "Who is she?"

"Her name is Grace Deveraux. She was reported missing by her family six months ago. Nobody has seen her for months."

I feel my heart start to beat faster at his words. *How can this be? This is the woman Dean has been having an affair with, the one in the picture I saw before he attacked me.*

"Dean used to work for the Deveraux family before his stroke. She is the woman he was having an affair with." I step away and start to pace as my brain whirls with pieces of the puzzle and yet I can't piece them together to make it all fit.

"Did they find her?"

"No, but I have people on this. I won't let anything happen to you, Lexi."

I stop at his words and move to him so that we are close, barely touching but the connection we share is so strong it's like an electric current pulls us together.

"I know you won't, but you can't be with us all the time. You have people to hire and fire and deals to make and small countries to overthrow," I say with a laugh to lighten my words.

"Overthrow countries," he says with a belly laugh that makes his handsome face look free.

"Well, I don't know what you do, do I. I'm just a small fry in the small business sector. You are a titan of industry."

His face sobers, but the twinkle is still there. "Would you like to know what I do?"

"Hell, yes."

"Okay, let me phone down and have the car brought to the front." He places a call to someone called Adam. I grab my jacket and shrug it on.

"Before we go, there is something I want to talk to you about." He takes my hands and leads me to the couch. I sit beside him as he looks at me, his face is serious. "I have a security team guarding the shop, and your house and you will have someone with you at all times, even to run to the store when I'm not with you. They come highly recommended by a friend of mine. I know it's not ideal but—"

I stop him with my finger on his lips. "It's okay, I understand and actually it makes me feel better to know the people I care about are safe."

"So, no arguments?"

I shake my head. "No arguments."

I see his shoulders sag infinitesimally as if he has been worried about my reaction.

"I just hope the police find Dean and Grace soon, I don't want this hanging over us when Junior is born," I say.

Hunter is silent. There is nothing we can say about that, we both want it, but we also know it is looking less likely as the police haven't found a trace of Dean.

I spend the rest of the day with Hunter at the Lungo Headquarters. The people are nice and genuinely friendly, although I don't see his friend Jake for which I'm glad. I'm not in the mood for a confrontation with him right now.

Hunter interacts with his staff in a polite, respectful manner, but you can still see who is in charge. There is a quiet authority about him, an aura of power and vitality that exudes off him. It's raw, and sexy as hell. He knows everyone by name from the mailroom staff to the director of finance. Everyone defers to him. He shows me the businesses they own, and what comes under the umbrella of Lungo Corp. What projects they are currently working on and what they see happening in the future. It's fun and more exciting than I thought it would be, but I realize it's being with him and seeing the excitement he has for what he does that I enjoy.

It is just him. I had hoped to protect my heart from Hunter but now I know I never stood a chance, because he already owned it.

IT HAS BEEN three days since the incident with Grace Devereaux and there has been no news from the police. Hunter has his people working on it and I'm hopeful they will find something. I'm living with him in the Penthouse.

I have no interest in going back to my house. It has been tainted to such a degree that I don't want to ever set foot in there again.

Cherry has brought me all the things I need for an extended stay, including my maternity bag. It sits in the corner of the room, ready and waiting for when I need it. Hunter and I haven't spoken about the future and what might happen when all of this is over. Part of me wants to ask him and the other part wants us to coast along, not facing the future that is so unknown right now.

I've decided to go back to the shop tomorrow, and while it's been lovely living in a bubble with Hunter, it's time to get back to normal. I also don't want Dean to think he has driven me from my life. My shame is fading, and a sense of anger is making me strong now. I won't let him drive me from the shop I love. He can drive me from the house, and I have instructed Move4You to handle everything, but he will not take the business I spent hours killing myself for. No way. I have been introduced to my security detail. Derrick is a tall muscular man who looks to be ex-special forces and Tanner is a retired cop. Both men are friendly but reserved. It is weird to think they are being paid to sit outside my shop and watch my every move.

I'm soaking in a bubble bath when I hear the door open. I know it's Hunter as he texted me earlier to say what time he would be in.

"Lex?" he calls.

"In here!" I shout back.

He walks into the bathroom, his eyes instantly raking over every inch of my body like a sensual caress. His eyes darken to almost navy as he focuses on the way the water bobs around the rounded curve of my breasts.

"Like what you see?" I ask emboldened by his gaze. I can see he does by the hard ridge in his dark gray slacks. Hunter tugs at the red tie around his neck before he starts to quickly shed the rest of his clothes.

"Oh, I more than like it, I fucking love it," he says as he stalks to the bath like a hunter on the prowl, removing his clothes as he does. I shiver with expectation as he steps in behind me, caging me with his hard body, his legs either side of mine as he pulls me back, so I lay with my back on his chest.

I feel the hardness of his erection as it presses into my back and heat floods my pussy as my nipples tingle with need.

He is determined to torture me as he picks up a sponge and proceeds to cover it in soap before using it to wash my shoulders and neck, he swirls the sponge around my body as he asks me about my day. He knows what he's doing, I can hardly hold a thought let alone speak about my day.

I lean my head back so that he has better access to my body, the sight of his big tanned hands against the paler skin of my full breasts make me press my legs together as desire hits me hot and hard in my clit.

He rolls my nipples that are so tender and sensitive between his thumb and forefinger and I arch into him with a groan that is torn from my lips.

"What do you need, Lex?" he asks. I hear the barely veiled desire in his husky voice. His hand moves over my round belly, with an almost reverence in his touch.

"You're so fucking beautiful like this. I feel like I could stay buried inside you forever and it would never be enough." His words ignited a fire in me.

"Hunter?"

"Um?"

"Stop torturing me."

His soft chuckle in my ear makes me squirm, but my words have the desired effect. I feel his finger slip between my lips finding my entrance as it glances over my clit. I'm so sensitized by his touch that I know it will take barely anything for me to climax. His finger penetrates me, and I feel my hips move as if they have a mind of their own, moving, seeking release in a rhythm as old as time.

"That's it, Lex, fuck yourself on my fingers," he whispers close to my ear, before biting down on the tender lobe. His words are like an accelerant, making the fire burn brighter as he begins to rub circles on my clit with his thumb. Light flits behind my closed eyelids as I feel my orgasm start to build, rising, rising until I teeter on the peek between two worlds. Reality ceases to exist as only feeling and sensation matter before I fall, shattering as every nerve in my body explodes in a powerful climax. I feel his fingers and the way my body squeezes him tight. As I start to come down his fingers gentle on me.

"Fuck you're magnificent," he says as he turns my head for a heated kiss.

I'm boneless as he kisses me. He pulls away, standing and stepping from the bath, his body like that of a Greek god, water running down the chiseled tanned muscle. He is beautiful, masculine, and strong and he makes my mouth water.

All too soon he is covering himself with a towel before he helps me stand and wraps me in a bath sheet. Not expecting it, I let out a little shriek when he sweeps me into his arms and carries me to the bed we now share. He dries me with tenderness before helping me into one of his t-shirts. I can see he is aroused, but he makes no mention of it as he pulls on boxers.

"How about some food?"

"I could eat," I shrug. I'm too distracted by this man to eat but we are still new, and I don't want to seem like a sex-starved maniac.

"Good. You're gonna need your energy. I have plans for this sexy body," he says with a sexy wink as he walks from the room. I smile to myself. *Oh yeah, tonight is going to be fun.*

CHAPTER FOURTEEN

LEXI

"SERIOUSLY, I CAN'T BELIEVE HE WILL BE HERE IN JUST two weeks," Cherry says as she rests her hand on my moving bump. I'm thirty-eight weeks pregnant and the last few months have been almost perfect. I say almost perfect because the only blot on my landscape is that there has been no sign of Dean or Grace.

It would almost be better if they had been spotted. Living with this hanging over my head, this constant sense of awareness is draining. I dismiss the negative thoughts and smile at my friend. "I know, I'm so excited but also terrified. Can you believe I have two weeks before having to push a watermelon out of my vagina!" I say in mock horror.

"I know. Poor Hunter. It's going to be like dipping his dick in the ocean when you next have sex," she giggles.

"Hey!" I laugh as I smack her on the arm lightly. "What about me? I've heard some horror stories about childbirth. Let me tell you, women are not shy about sharing their horror stories when they hear you are expecting. It's almost like a competition to see who can tell the worst birthing story." Cherry is laughing with abandon now. "I'm serious, these people are evil, the home births are the worst. They get the whole family round to watch. It's crazy. I've already told Hunter he is staying at the top, I'm not having him see that."

We were sitting in the living room at Hunter's Penthouse going over some designs for a big commission due to start next year. We have agreed that I will take six months off to be with the baby, only dipping my toe in when needed and we will take on someone who is just as qualified.

"So, I will advertise for someone tomorrow now we have agreed," Cherry says with a sad look.

"What's up, Fairy?"

"I don't know. It's like the end of an era, not working together every day, you having the baby. It just makes me a little sad. Don't get me wrong, I'm so happy for you, you deserve every bit of happiness you have, and I love you with Hunter."

"I'll be coming back to work," I say as I take her hand.

"I know, I'm just being silly."

"I'm glad you like Hunter and I know you will find your own Hunter."

Cherry snorted. "Men like Hunter are as rare as horse shit that smells good."

I laugh at that wondering how he would react to that comparison.

"What about Jake?" I ask softly. Cherry has been tight-lipped about what happened with them and I have tried not to push. But ever since they saw each other at Lungo

HQ, she has been acting weird. Her face falls, and she drops her head not looking me in the eye.

"What about him? He is ancient history."

"Is he? Because it doesn't feel like he is."

Her head comes up and a hardness that I hadn't seen before is there. "We dated, he broke my heart, end of story. I wouldn't spit on him if he was on fire now," she vows and we both know it wasn't that simple, but I won't push.

"Okay, so as soon as chunk here is born our new mission is to find you a hot man." I smile, then wince as an extra strong Braxton hicks contraction ripples through my belly.

"You okay?"

"Yeah just Braxton hicks. They have been strong all day. My body is practicing apparently."

"Well, on that note, I have to go." Cherry stands and I hold out my hand.

"Pull me up." When I'm up I walk her to the door. "What time is your flight?

"Six pm." Cherry was going to look at some artwork for the shop and was flying to New York.

"Okay, call me when you get there."

We hug, and I close the door. It was only eleven-thirty. Hunter had gone to do a workout with Jake. The two needed to rebuild their relationship, so I'd suggested he call him when he mentioned going to the gym. The gym incidentally was in the basement of this building. Hunter never went far from me except to go to work. He never said it, but he was worried about Dean and Grace disappearing.

I knew he was keeping things about the case from me, he'd said as much, even asking if I wanted all the details.

At the time I said no as I didn't want the increased stress hurting my baby. I trusted that if it was pertinent he would tell me.

I wonder if I should have a quick bath while I wait for Hunter to come back and get me. We are supposed to be at his parent's house by two for lunch. Maybe the warm water will ease my backache.

Stripping, I run the warm water before letting myself sink into its soothing heat. My hair is in a bun on top of my head, so I sink down low letting the water lap over my skin. As I lay there letting the bath ease my back I think about Cherry and the way she had looked when she'd talked about Jake. I wonder if I should ask Hunter about it but then thought maybe I shouldn't as their relationship was still on thin ice.

I hated that I had inadvertently caused a rift in their friendship. The sensible part of me knew it wasn't my fault but the other part knew if it wasn't for me, it wouldn't have happened.

Feeling the water cool, I stand, noticing the ache had gone. I step from the bath and wrap a bath sheet around me. My wardrobe options are limited so I don't have to take ages pouring over outfits.

I'm pulling panties out of the drawer when I hear Hunter come in.

"Lex!"

"Through here."

He walks in looking hot and sweaty in black gym shorts and a white gym top. His body glistening, his muscles pumped from his work out. I lick my lips as I look at all the deliciousness in front of me.

"Lexi," he growls, and my head whips up. His eyes are dark navy as they sear into me, he looks powerful and so fucking masculine. I'm not sure if it is pregnancy or just Hunter, but I want him all the time.

His voice is guttural as he rasps out the next words. "Lexi if you keep looking at me like that we're going to be late for lunch with my parents."

I think about that for maybe half a second. "Or you could stop talking and wasting time and get your ass over here?" I say.

He is in front of me in seconds, pulling the towel away from my now dry body. He steps back slightly so he can look at me. Hunter loves looking at me, at first, I had been shy about it especially with all the changes in my body. But he made me feel beautiful and sexy so now I let him take his fill.

"So fucking beautiful," he moans as he runs a finger from my temple, all the way down over my heavy breast then over my huge belly until he reaches my pussy. He drags a finger through my lips and I know what he will find.

"Always wet for me," he murmurs as he uses the same finger to spread the wetness from my core to the bundle of nerves that drives me wild. I let my head fall back as he teases me until I'm on the brink, time and again. He stops and sheds his gym clothes until he is standing in front of me gloriously naked, his thick erection straining toward his chiseled belly.

Stepping forward he kissed me hard, nipping at my lip until I moaned from the bite.

"Such a naughty girl, teasing me like this," he moans, and I smile into the kiss. Gently he turns me around, careful to make sure I'm steady before he pushes my shoulders gently so that I'm leaning on the dressing table. I see him come behind me in the mirror, his eyes heated with desire.

"So sexy," he whispers as he pushes into me. My body arches toward him as he begins to fuck me with one hand on my shoulder to hold me steady, the other gentle on my hip. Our eyes hold, locked in the moment as he fucks me harder and harder, but still with restraint, knowing he fights for control because he doesn't want to hurt our son only makes me love him more.

Higher and higher he brings us until we both crest the peak, our climaxes hitting us, blinding us only to each other as hearts and minds meld into one giant sensation of feeling. My body spasms around him as he spills into me, making everything more intense. Even after he is done he stays inside me as he plants soft kisses up my spine.

"I love you, Lex,"

I find his eyes in the mirror, the emotion in them almost making me cry with the love I feel for this man. How could I have thought I loved Dean? What I felt for him was nothing compared to the earth-shattering feelings I feel for Hunter.

CHAPTER FIFTEEN

LEXI

"WE'RE ONLY FIVE MINUTES LATE," I SAY, NOW regretting being late. What would his mother think? Vivian was everything a Southern woman should be. I bet she was never late because of a romp in the hay.

We come to a stop outside Hank and Vivian's home. I've only been here once before when we came for dinner one night a few weeks ago. The house is huge and grand and suits the McKenzie's perfectly. That was the night I also met Cassie and her adorable daughter Mellie. They had all been charming, friendly, and warm. It was lovely having them in my life, especially since I haven't seen my own mother for months.

My parents promise to come over when the baby is born, they had tried to get away, but my aunt isn't well, and they are needed to help with my grandmother. I understand but it doesn't mean I don't miss them. I'm also anxious for Hunter to meet them.

Hunter guides me from the car, his hand on the small

of my back, as we approach the door. Pushing through we are met with silence.

"Mom said they might fire up the grill so maybe they are outback," he says with a nod to the door for me to proceed him.

I step through the door and almost scream.

"Surprise," a chorus of voices shout. In front of me stood Vivian and Hank, Cherry, Darla, Frank, Jake, Cassie, and *oh my God*, my parents. I turn to look at Hunter, tears in my eyes.

"You did this? You brought my parents over?"

He grins and swipes at my tears. "I had some help," he winks as he kissed me softly. "Go see them." He nods toward my mom and dad who have pushed to the front. My dad has tears in his eyes as did my mom as we all embraced.

"Oh, my God, I've missed you so much," I cry. My mom sobs, and my dad laughs.

"Oh, my princess, look at you," my father says as he hugs me tightly. I breath in the familiar scent of my dad and tears run anew.

"I can't believe you are here." I laugh as I feel Hunter's hand on my back. I turn to him with a smile, mouthing thank you. He nods and then lets me go as I'm embraced by Vivian and Hank, Darla, Frank, and Cherry.

"You little sneak," I say as we hug.

"Well, I had to keep you busy, so Hunter could run around all morning collecting your parents while Vivian and Cassie helped Darla and Frank."

I look around the patio which is decorated with baby blue streamers, cream and blue flower bouquets—which on closer inspection are made from tiny socks rolled into roses. White balloons are tied to the end of a table which is filled with baby themed canapes with a huge white cake covered in pale blue and lemon ribbon and a tiny fondant elephant in the middle.

I walk around taking it all in, hearing the people I love chatter and I've never felt so much love. My son will be so lucky to have these people in his life. I rub my belly thinking how this child I carry brought us all together.

"Lexi," I turn at the sound of a man's voice.

"It's Jake, right?" I ask knowing it was. He looks unsure, ill at ease, but handsome in a devilish boy-next-door way. I can see why Cherry had fallen for him.

"Yes. I just wanted to apologize for my behavior at the office that day. I was a complete asshole and behaved despicably."

"Well, I'd love to disagree but...,"

I say with a grin. He returns my grin with one of his own.

"I was a dick, but it wasn't personal. I thought I was protecting my friend, but I was just jealous. I see that now. For what it's worth, I really am happy he has someone who makes him so happy."

"Why jealous?" I ask with my head tilted as I wait for his answer.

He shuffles from one foot to the next looking uncomfortable. "He's my best friend, my wingman and I didn't want that to change. It was selfish and childish. He has the right to be happy with the woman he loves."

"And what about you?" I ask knowing I was probably way overstepping.

"Me? I think my chance is lost," he says wistfully as he looks off at something to my right. I turn and see Cherry laughing with Cassie, her pink hair in a perfect forties wave, she is glamorous and beautiful.

"You never know what the future holds, Jake," I say with a grin.

"Friends?" he asks as he holds out his hand.

"Friends" I say. As I go to take his hand I feel a gush of liquid between my legs. I look down and gasp. "Oh no." I'm still holding Jakes' hand and just squeeze it tight as pain hits me in my lower abdomen.

"What is it?" he asks looking terrified as I double over.

"My water just broke," I gasp as I look around for Hunter. At that second, he looks up from talking with my father and our eyes lock. I see his worried expression as he runs over to me.

"Lexi," he says pushing Jake out of the way as he wraps his arm around me.

I look up at him as my pain eases and smile. "We're having a baby,"

"I know that, Lex," he says as if I was telling him the obvious.

"No, I mean my water broke, we are having a baby now."

I see him gulp as his eyes go wide. "Fuck, we're having a baby," he shouts to the entire room.

CHAPTER SIXTEEN

LEXI

"I HEAR WE'RE HAVING A BABY," DR. O'CONNOR SAYS AS he walks into the room with a warm, professional smile.

"Yes, my water broke about an hour ago." He stands beside me as I lie on the bed, Hunter beside me.

Dr. O'Connor is looking at the monitors as he speaks. "Any contractions?"

"Yes, they started right away and seem to be quite regular."

"Any backache?"

"A little last night and this morning."

"You never said anything," Hunter accuses.

I look at his worried face and shrug. "I thought it was normal."

"Well, some backache, but it can also be a sign of labor. Let's get you checked and see how things are progressing."

I nod but don't speak as another contraction grips me.

Dr. O'Connor places his palm on my belly as he watches the monitor. "Just breath through it, Lexi. Well done, it will soon be over," he says in a calm authoritative voice.

I practice my breathing as I gripped Hunter's hand and feel the contraction start to wane.

"That was a nice strong one." He turns to the midwife beside me. "How often is she contracting?"

"Every two minutes."

He nods. "Okay let's take a look at you."

The next few minutes are not the greatest of my life as Dr. O'Connor proceeds to give me an internal exam to determine how far dilated I am. I look at Hunter who is calm and in control.

He smiles a reassuring smile and kisses my hand. "You're doing great, Lex. I'm so proud of you."

"Okay," Dr. O'Connor says as he takes off the latex glove and tosses it away. "You're five centimeters dilated, and fifty percent effaced. Looks like those back pains were doing some work after all. Would you like anything for the pain?"

I nod already having decided that pain was not for me. "Yes please."

"Okay, I'll write something up for you. I will be on site and can be paged if I'm needed but for now, I'll leave you in the capable hands of Mari."

"Thank you," I murmur as another contraction hits.

Mari leaves with Dr. O'Connor and as she opens the door I see the waiting area is full of people. My mom, dad, Vivian and Hank, Cherry, Darla, Frank, Cassie and even Jake is there.

"Did they follow us here?" I ask when the contraction subsides enough for me to speak.

"They sure did. Our family is anxious to meet this little

guy." He places a hand on my belly and rubs gently. "Can you believe this is happening?"

"As it's my body that currently feels like it is getting ripped apart, yes, I do," I chuckle.

The next few hours are a constant stream of contractions that are getting more and more painful until I think I can't take any more. The drugs I was given barely put a dent in the pain and I'm sucking on the oxygen as if it's a lifeline.

Dr. O'Connor walks in and he has changed into scrubs. "I hear we are ready to start pushing." He smiles as he takes a seat on a moving stool and positions himself at the business end of the table. "Okay, on your next contraction I need you to bear down like we talked about. Okay, here it comes."

I spend the next half an hour pushing until the sweat is pouring off me and I'm exhausted. I lay back as the contraction eases away and feel like weeping. I turn to look at Hunter who has not left my side the entire time. He mops my brow with a cool cloth, the other hand squeezed in mine.

"I can't do this," I say wearily.

"Yes, you can. You are the strongest woman I know, and you can do this. I'm right here, Lex. I love you so much and our little boy is nearly here."

His words fortify me. I've been through so much and I would walk through fire for my son. The next contraction is a doozy and I push with all my might as I scream through the pain while Hunter and Dr. O'Connor encourage me.

"That's great, Lexi, the head is out."

Everything happens quickly after that and then with blessed relief, I feel my son come into the world. An instant cry from him makes me sob out a cry of emotion as I look to Hunter who has tears running down his face as our beautiful son is placed on my chest.

He has a shock of dark hair, and an adorable scrunched up face. I hold him to me as Hunter places his hand over the top of mine, the other around me as he holds us both. I count his tiny fingers and toes.

"So, you're the one who has been kicking me," I whisper. The love I feel for my son is overwhelming, not like anything I have ever felt before. So different for the love I feel for Hunter.

"He's beautiful, Lex," he says with awe and emotion in his voice.

"He is, isn't he?" I whisper back. The room is a hive of activity, but we are in our own little bubble. "Can you believe we made him?"

"No, it's surreal to think how this started. Now I have the love of my life and a gorgeous son who already owns my heart just from being here."

I look at Hunter and he kisses me lightly.

"Thank you, Lex, for giving me this gift. I won't let either of you down." It is a vow he makes to us both and it is one I know he has no intention of breaking.

CHAPTER SEVENTEEN

HUNTER

I HOLD MY SON IN MY ARMS AS THEY CLEAN LEXI UP, MY gaze on the tiny being in my arms. The love I feel for him is nothing like I have ever felt before. I know that I would die for this child to protect him. A feeling of absolute joy fills me when he opens his sleepy eyes and looks straight at me.

"Hey, little guy, I'm your daddy." My son's answer is to shove his fist in his mouth, although his aim is a little off. I smile. I know that he is going to bring me a lifetime of joy. Watching him grow, teaching him to ride a bike, watching as he becomes a man. He closes his eyes and I hand him back to Lexi who is now cleaned up. She has never looked more beautiful than she does right now.

Her hair is damp, her face exhausted but the serene smile and the look of absolute adoration on her face when she looks at us makes my heart squeeze. I never thought I could love her more but, at this moment, I know that I will feel that way every day that I'm alive and even afterward.

Every moment with her by my side is a treasure that I cherish, every smile, every loving look. It is something that I hadn't been looking for but now it is something that I know I can't live without.

"I need to go tell our entourage," I say with a quick kiss to her head. "I won't be gone long. Do you want to see anyone?"

"Yes, let them in. I'm ready to show off this little guy."

"He needs a name," I say as I look at her. We had briefly discussed names but neither one of us could come up with any that we both loved.

"What about Theo Henry Cosmo McKenzie?" Lexi asks and once again I have the feeling that I can't love her more.

I look to our son who is sleeping contentedly against her breast and nod. "I think it's perfect." I lean in and kiss her head again.

I walk to the door and ease it open slipping out quietly. I can feel the grin that is splitting my face as everyone jumps up to greet me. My Mom and Dad, Lexi's parents—Cosmo, and Elena—all surround me.

"Is he here?" Cherry asks as I look to where she is standing beside Cassie.

"Yes, he is absolutely beautiful. Lexi did so well, and they are both fine." I answer their unasked questions. I'm hugged by my parents and then by Lexi's mom and dad before Cherry hugs me as she cries tears of joy.

"Thank you for making my friend so happy."

I hug her back and then she moves away as my sister, Darla, Frank, and Jake get in on the congratulatory hand-shakes and hugs. I'm truly overwhelmed by the amount of love for us both and I know in my heart that my son will be loved beyond compare by the people in this room.

"Can we see them?" Elena asks.

"Yes, of course, she wants to see you all." I open the door and proceed them in as I take my place next to Lexi. Oohs and aahs are exclaimed by the people we love about what a beautiful baby he is and how much hair he has. Tears of joy are cried— more hugs are passed out.

"What are you calling him?" Cosmo asks.

Lexi looks at me with a nod and a grin. "Theo Henry Cosmo McKenzie," I announce as we both watch our father's reactions.

They are the men who made us who we are, it is only right that he bears their names. Gasps of delight are heard around the room. I see both men look first at Theo and then Lexi and me. My father has a sheen of tears in his eyes as he turns to Cosmo who has tears running down his face. The two men shake hands.

"Thank you," my father says as he moves to me. "It is such an honor."

"Would you like to hold him?"

"Yes please." My father sits in the chair beside Lexi and I scoop our son into my arms and hand him over. The look of love I see in his eyes touches me deeply. My father is the greatest man I know, and if I can be half the father he is I will be happy.

"How much does he weigh?" Cherry asks as she leans over my dad and touches Theo's tiny fingers.

"He was a whopping nine pounds, four ounces," Lexi replies.

"Wow, my ocean comment wasn't far off," she laughs.

I make a mental note to ask Lexi later what that means. Jake is hanging back, looking like he doesn't know how to act, and I hate that. If today has taught me anything it's that we need these people in our lives. I can't stay angry with him for wanting to protect me and I can't say I would have done things differently in his position.

I squeeze Lexi's hand gently and nod toward Jake. She smiles a look of understanding.

I approach Jake and stand beside him. "Got a second?" I ask as I nod to the door.

I see the look of awkwardness move to one of resignation as he precedes me out. I walk down the corridor a little and then sit in the chairs that they have occupied for hours as they waited for Theo to enter the world.

"I know what you're going to say, Mac. I just wanted to see that the baby and Lexi were okay. I'll leave you in peace now," he says as he looks at me.

Jake and I have been friends for so long, he is like a brother to me and I hate that he thinks I want him gone.

He turns to leave, and I call him back. "Jake, just wait a sec."

He stops and turns, a surly look on his face. "Why? So, you can tell me what an asshole I've been? I know that okay, and I have apologized to Lexi. I was a douche bag and I have no excuse."

"You were a dick, but I could have handled things better too. The thing is, Lexi comes first, and you cross her then you cross me. That said, this whole year has been fucked up with one thing or another. Yes, you messed up but I'm ready to put it behind us if you are." I watch him process my words. Jake is notoriously stubborn.

He breaks out in a grin and offers his hand. I take it and we shake hands. I feel the tension leave my body. I hate falling out with Jake but I'm not sorry I did, he needs to know that we have new boundaries—he upsets Lexi then he upsets me.

"So, you're a dad now. Does that mean you're going to get boring and start drinking wheatgrass smoothies instead of coming out with me?"

"Fuck off, Jake. I've never touched a wheatgrass smoothie in my life and I don't intend to start now," I say as we move toward the door. "Why don't we talk about the way you keep looking at Cherry."

I see him roll his eyes but not before pain crosses them. "Yeah, okay, point taken. Can we just go coo over your son instead?"

"Sure, let's do that." I laugh as I follow him back inside.

Lexi instantly seeks me out and I can see she is exhausted. She would never admit it and she is smiling so big. I offer her a reassuring smile before I turn to the group looking for my son. This need to know where he is and if he is safe feels new but at the same time old. It is ingrained in me as smoothly as breathing.

He is nestled in Elena's arms as she looks at him with all the love and devotion of a grandmother. I smile to myself as I sit beside Lexi, taking her hand.

"You okay?" I ask leaning in close to her.

"Yes, I'm perfect." She replies with a tired smile.

"I think Lex is tired guys," I say as I stand. The fact that she does not contradict me proves how tired she is.

"Yes, let's leave this little family to it," my mom says. More hugs and kisses are exchanged. "We should go and eat the baby shower cake and celebrate," she says, and the others agree.

I love the thought that they are celebrating together

even as I see Jake and Cherry glaring at each other with barely contained hate.

I dismiss them from my mind as I settle my son in Lexi's arms. He starts to route around looking for food so with the practiced ease that seems to be passed down from eons of women, she opens her nightgown and helps our son latch onto her breast. Had I known how profoundly this would affect me I would have given every cent I had to have this moment in time paused for infinity. My throat is clogged with the strength of feelings I feel in this moment. Love, fear, doubt, joy all mingle in me to form a snapshot in time that will be the pinnacle of when my life changed. It is a moment I will reflect on when I'm old and gray, surrounded by my children and grandchildren and know this was the moment when my life really began.

CHAPTER EIGHTEEN

LEXI

THE LATE AFTERNOON SUN SHINES ON MY FACE, THE breeze from the ocean ruffling my hair as I walk beside Hunter, our hands entwined. Theo is nestled securely in a baby carrier against his daddy's chest, fed and content he sleeps without a care in the world.

At seven weeks old my baby boy has just experienced his first family vacation. It is our last night at Hunter's house in the Hamptons. I didn't even realize that Hunter owned a property in the Hampton's, but it shouldn't have surprised me. The house was right on the beach. Glass across the back made the best of the spectacular views. A mix of modern and classic touches inside made it feel luxurious and yet still homely. Lots of cream and neutral tones in with blues and sea greens making you feel like the beach extended inside the house.

Our bodyguards were still there but they were so good that we could hardly see them unless we looked. It was the only reminder of the danger that was still out there. We haven't heard a thing from Dean and part of me hopes he has moved on. I have a meeting with my divorce lawyer next to see if I can move ahead without him being present. I'm brought from my thoughts by Hunter.

"What would you like to do tonight?" He asks as we near the end of the private section of beach.

I lean into his shoulder, sneaking a look at Theo who is dozing off after his last feeding. He is such a good baby, he hardly cries and only wakes at night to eat. My boy is a hungry one and when he wants to eat he makes sure everyone knows about it. Thanks to his appetite and the fact that I'm breastfeeding, I have shed most of my baby weight.

Like most people did though I'd assumed I would go back to my original shape. I haven't yet, my tummy though flat now was certainly not as firm as it had been and I'm sure my ass wobbled more now too. Hunter apparently loves my new body as much as my old one. But I know it is different. I've always been confident about my body and it is taking some adjustment to love this new me.

"I don't know," I reply after a beat.

"How about I grill some steaks and we spend the evening in the jacuzzi when he goes down?" he asks with a wiggle of his eyebrows.

I burst out laughing and nod before going up on tiptoes to kiss my man before replying. "Okay, Mr. Transparent."

"I can't help that I want you all the time," he replies as he pulls me closer, his arm going around my back as we make our way back to the house over the sand dunes.

"Whatever." I laugh secretly pleased that he still finds

me desirable. After my six weeks check-up I thought I would feel self-conscious when Hunter made love to me, but he eased all my fears and made it perfect for me. He'd known how nervous I was and made sure I knew how much he loved me and how beautiful he found me.

The last seven weeks have been the happiest of my life. My mom and dad stayed for three weeks reveling in their time with Theo and I. Hank and Vivian had been wonderful and I hadn't realized when I met Hunter how I would also be gaining another family in them.

"Do you want to take a nap while I bathe and change Theo?" Hunter asks.

"I might just read a while," I reply offering my mouth for another kiss, which he gives me. His kisses make my body hum with desire. I wonder if there will ever be a time when I don't want him, that I won't feel my heart flutter when he walks in a room. I can't imagine it ever happening. We burn so bright and so hot, but we are so in complete sync with everything. It is difficult to remember how messed up our start was. Now it seems like we have always been together, and I wonder if perhaps it is because we were always meant to be together.

I'm sitting on the back deck, facing the beach when a text pings on my phone. I pick it up and open it with a smile thinking it will be Cherry. My heart stutters as I see the image that has come through from an unknown number.

It is a picture of Hunter and me from last night at the seafood restaurant near the dock. The stroller is beside Hunter as he rocks Theo while we eat. Hunter's face has been scrubbed out and, in its place, is Dean's image. My hand shakes and my breathing hitches as I read the accompanying text.

. . .

UNKNOWN: *Soon we will be a family.*

I THROW THE PHONE DOWN. My immediate reaction is to call for Hunter, but I don't want to ruin our last night together. I sit and listen while he talks to Theo as he gives him his bath. They love this time together—Theo smiles and kicks his legs with glee when he gets in the water. Should I say anything, or should I let us have this last night without the pain of my past ruining it?

My gut says I should tell Hunter about the text, miscommunication is what got us into a mess in the first place. Tears hit the back of my throat as anger floods me. *Fucking Dean and his fucked-up shit.* I hate him so much and yet sometimes it is hard to separate the man he is now with the sweet man that I married.

How can one person be two different people and how did I not know it? It plagues me. Even now sometimes a sliver of doubt will creep in about Hunter and whether I can trust what I know about him. The big difference is that Hunter has a big family and friends that talk about him every chance they get and bring out baby pictures at every opportunity.

I never saw a single baby picture of Dean and apart from his parents who were distant to say the least, I never met anyone from before we met. He always said it was because they moved around a lot and his parents were only children but now I doubt that to be true.

I decide to tell Hunter tomorrow and to enjoy our last night on our first family vacation. I lift my head as Hunter walks out of the bathroom with Theo wrapped in a towel.

I force the smile on my face to look natural, not wanting him to see I'm upset.

Hunter stops dead as he approaches me, his eyes on my face. "What's wrong?"

I should have known I wouldn't be able to hide it from him. He is always in tune with my mood, I can't hide from him and maybe I shouldn't try.

"I got a text," I say as I stand and move to pick up my phone from where I threw it.

"And?" he asks. I can feel the hum of vibration as he waits for my answer. He knows that whatever am about to say is bad.

"I thought it was Cherry, so I didn't check who it was. When I opened it, there was a picture and a message." I hand him the phone as I take Theo from him, cradling his tiny, warm body against my chest. I watch his face for a reaction and his jaw goes rigid with fury, his eyes are almost black with it. The phone cracks as he grips it so hard his knuckles turn white.

"I'm going to fucking kill him," he snarls and for a second, I believe he will. "Go inside and pack Lex. We're leaving and don't tell anyone we're coming home. I don't want to give this fucker a heads up."

"Do you think someone is telling him?" I ask, and I can't hide the fear as I hug my son to me, rocking back and forth not knowing who I'm comforting—my son or myself. Hunter hears the worry in my voice and crosses to me quickly. Before I know it, I'm in his arms held tight against his chest as he kisses my head. Just his arms around me, gives me comfort and strength. His scent all around me offers a sense of security.

"Don't worry, Lex, we'll get him."

I feel the promise in his words but the shiver that runs

through me makes me look out over the beach. It is empty, but I can't help but feel I'm being watched now.

"Go pack, I need to make some calls and then we'll leave."

I go inside and do as he asks and pray that my perfect life will not be stolen from me.

CHAPTER NINETEEN

HUNTER

I LIE ON OUR BED IN THE PENTHOUSE AND WATCH LEXI as she sleeps. The tiny crease lines of worry are gone from her eyes. The last few days have been tough on her, things moved fast after she got the threatening text. Within hours we were on my private plane flying home. The thought that Dean had been so close to her and my son makes my blood boil with rage. I can't ever remember feeling such hatred for anyone.

I had hoped this would all be over by now, but it seems Dean Crane or Dean Crouch as he really was, is better at hiding than we knew.

How do you tell the woman you loved that everything she knew about the man she married was wrong? But Dean has made his move and poked his head out of the hole he'd been hiding in and we were closing in. I don't care if he ends up dead or in prison for the rest of his life just as long as he never gets the chance to put fear in Lexi's eyes again.

It had been a little shocking for me to find out that he had such a dark past. Even now, the psychologist's reports make me shiver. I must have read the report a dozen times trying to wrap my head around it.

Born Dean David Crouch, he'd shown early signs of Psychosis. At the age of six, the neighbor's accused him of setting fire to their chicken coop. His then adoptive parents had sold their house and moved from Florida to New York to start a new life. I feel half sorry for them, they thought they were helping a kid get out of the system after his junkie mother dumped him off before overdosing. What they got was a seriously disturbed child and a life-time of running.

As a young teen he'd been accused of arson, assault on a teacher and diagnosed with antisocial personality disorder with narcissistic tendencies. It was later diag-nosed as Psychopathic with narcissist tendencies. In one of the reports, the doctor had noted that Dean had the ability to charm and hold down relatively normal relation-ships until he was cornered or felt as if he didn't get the attention he was due. He commented that he feels that Dean posed a threat to himself and others.

His parents managed to get that buried. His adoptive father was a senior judge and used his connections to have the reports buried. Then they moved to Ohio where Dean began college and met Lexi. Funnily enough, that had proven to be the longest period of stability in Dean's life, or so it seemed.

I've received word from my contact that Grace Devereaux had been reported missing by her family six months ago, something the police didn't tell me. I feel bad for keeping things from Lexi but before Theo was born it seemed like the best decision, the extra strain would have done her no good and then afterward there never seemed like there was a good time.

Now as I watch her sleep I know the time is coming when she must be told the truth so that she can fully understand the danger Dean poses. The sun is coming up when I heard the snuffles from the baby monitor that signal our son is waking. With a smile I slip from the bed and move down the hallway to the nursery.

Walking closer I see he is awake. I feel the grin spread across my face as I look at him. He has his mom's eyes and lips and my nose and skin tone. His fluffy jet-black hair is mine too.

"Hey, buddy," I say lifting him from the crib. His diaper is soaking wet, so I quickly change him. He starts to fuss, and I know I don't have much time before he decides he wants his breakfast. My boy likes his food and being cuddled by his mommy is his favorite place.

"You're a clever boy, aren't you? I would spend all day cuddled up to mommy too if I could," I say as I carry him to our room.

Lexi is sitting up, looking adorably disorientated as I sit beside her. Immediately Theo starts to cry, and Lexi puts her arms out for him. In seconds she has him latched on to her breast, feeding away contentedly. I honestly don't know if I have ever seen a more beautiful sight, but I feel like that all the time around her. The little serene smile that graces her lips seems to hold secrets and promises that would make a painter weep with joy.

I kiss her head before I grab a towel and head for the bathroom.

"Do you want eggs and toast when I'm done?" I ask as I lean against the door jam.

She looks up with a tilt of her head and purses her lips.

"Just toast, please. Do you have to go into the office today?"

I nod an affirmative. "Yes, just for the morning, then I have a meeting here to go over our security measures. I want you to meet Jack Granger, he will be handling this for me personally."

"Okay," she replies as if talking about security and personal protection is the norm. My girl takes everything in her stride.

I shower and when I come out, my son is over his mama's shoulder as she pats his back gently.

"Want me to take him while you shower?"

"Please. I feel gross," she says as she hands him over to me. She kisses his cheek and then holds the back of her hand to it and frowns.

"What's up?"

"He just feels a little warm. I'm sure it's nothing, but I'll keep an eye on him."

I continue patting Theo's butt until he lets out an almighty burp.

"Wow little guy," I say with a laugh as I lay him down on the bed while I dress. I slip on dark gray slacks, a white dress shirt with a vest, and loop a tie around my neck before throwing a clean burp cloth over my shoulder. I have learned my lesson with baby vomit down my back. As I head for the door, the bathroom door opens, and I can't help but stop. With wet hair dripping down her back, and her long lean legs on show, she is a dream, the scrap of towel barely covering her. I growl in my throat as I advance on her. Holding Theo in one arm, I slide the other around her back, anchoring her to me making the towel slip so her gorgeous nipples are peaking out.

"Fucking beautiful," I say and watch her blush.

Lexi loves my dirty mouth, but it always makes her blush. It's cute and it makes me hard. I kiss her hard, taking what I need from her, letting the moan from her travel down to my dick as she opens to me like the sweetest flower. I pull away and we are both breathless and flushed.

"Tonight," I say as I bend and whisper just what I want to do to her tonight in her ear. She shivers and clings to me. I want to strip her towel away and devour her, but my son won't hear of it and lets out a cry. I laugh as I pull away.

"Come on, son, we need to have a talk man to man."

Thirty minutes later I kiss both Lexi and Theo and leave for the office. I have a lot to get done but the most important is the meeting with Jack. We thought it best I meet him first and then Lexi meets him.

When I called him in to take care of Dean, I knew he and Eidolon could do the job. They have a reputation that is only found in certain military circles in the UK. A secret UK government organization, they were the people the military called when they couldn't get the job done.

Jack was Will Granger's brother and we met when Will did my tech security. I had been impressed with Will and made some inquiries that led to Jack turning up on my doorstep at midnight one night telling me to back off and stop looking, that I wouldn't get a second warning. The man was fucking terrifying and I didn't scare easily, but the fact that he could turn up on my penthouse balcony without coming through the door made me think twice about crossing him.

Instead of asking questions I offered him a whiskey and we got drunk while we argued about football. I woke the next morning with a hangover and a card with his number saying to call if I ever needed anything. So, I called.

It seemed like a no-brainer when the shit went down with Dean to call them. I didn't know too much, just that they were good, and that Jack had a soft spot for innocents getting hurt.

Jack had flown to the US as soon as this last incident happened and agreed to handle this personally. Now, we needed to meet as he had information he wanted to share personally.

CHAPTER TWENTY

HUNTER

As I stride to my office, opening the door with the key. My office is like a fortress. I have too many confidential papers in there to keep it open. I step through and stop dead as Jack reclines in my chair with a serious look on his face.

"Your security is crap," he says in a deadpan voice, his British accent making it sound even more so.

I hesitate before I move closer, we are two alpha males and while I like Jack, there is only room for one dog in this fight. I walk around to my chair and stand there as he looks up at me. We stare each other out and then Jack grins.

"Good to see you again, Hunter. Congrats on the kid," he says as he motions to a picture of Lexi and Theo on my desk.

We shake hands and I smile as Jack moves past me to the window. He is the kind of man who can't sit still, always moving, always watching.

"Thank you."

"I'm serious about your security though. I walked right in here with just a few flicks of my wrist and a wink at the girl on reception."

I huff out a breath. "It's that fucking accent." Which may be partly true but even I can see that Jack Granger is a handsome fucker and could probably charm the Queen of England out of her panties.

"We need to talk about Crane," he says as he moves to sit opposite me.

"I'm listening."

"We got word that a body has been found in a shallow grave in Clark State Forest. We have our system set up to look for things and this brought up a match. When we checked, it was confirmed that it was the body of Grace Devereaux."

I sucked in a breath and let it out on a curse. "Fuck!"

"Yeah, the poor girl was in a bad state. She had been raped and beaten before whoever killed her strangled her. We believe Crane killed her in a fit of rage and from our estimations she's been dead around six to seven weeks, but the autopsy report has not been completed."

"How come the police aren't here telling me this?" I say as I stand and start to pace.

"They only heard about ten minutes ago," he says looking at his watch with the fancy help and tracking app that Will had invented.

"Any sightings of Crane?"

"The last one was two days ago in the Hamptons. He has gone dark, but I fully suspect he will make his move any time now. I already have three of my men heading to your Penthouse. Alex, Decker, and Reid will take over from the guys you have covering Lexi and Theo."

My blood pumps as I feel the climax of this tense and scary situation coming to fruition. Just a few more days and it will all be over.

"Fine, let's head out and you can meet Lexi," I say as I stand and move for the door.

Just then my phone rings. My blood runs cold when I see all the missed calls from Lexi. I look at Jack who is frowning at his phone.

I dial the voicemail and listen as her voice comes on the line.

"Hunter, Theo has a fever. I tried calling you, but it keeps going to voicemail, so I'm going to go ahead and take him to the emergency room. I will let the guys know. Call me."

I let the phone slide down my side as a feeling of dread lands heavy in my belly.

"Mac, I just got word. My men found Lexi's car abandoned on the road toward Mariemont, no sign of her or Theo. The guys you had on Lexi are dead." The words ring in my ears as I feel a coldness sweep through my bones. Rage and fear hold me immobile as a roaring sound reverberates around me. It takes me a second to realize it is me. He has them. Dean has Lexi and Theo.

CHAPTER TWENTY-ONE

LEXI

WALKING OUT OF THE PEDIATRICIANS OFFICE WITH Theo in his baby carrier, I feel slightly foolish. I panicked when Theo was fussing and had a fever. I hadn't been able to get hold of Hunter, Vivian or Darla and decided to just take him to the clinic.

The doctor was wonderful and checked him over completely, before deciding it was a reaction to his vaccinations as everything seemed in perfect order. She reassured me it was normal and that if I had any more concerns to bring him back. After some Infant Tylenol, the fever seemed to come down quickly. Leaving the Doctors office, I let out a shaky breath. Having kids was a worry but a good one. I nod to the two bodyguards that were a step behind me. I quickly type a text to Hunter but then delete it, thinking I will call him when I get to the shop.

I want to go and see Cherry, so I decide to drive into Mariemont. I miss my house and the town I had grown up in. Despite only being an hour's drive it made such a huge difference. Everything was prettier here—Hunter and I had been looking at a few properties, but nothing had seemed right. So, until we found the perfect house we were staying in the penthouse.

I strapped Theo into the back of my car and got in the front knowing the guards would just follow. I was about five miles from the shop, singing along to an old Heart song when I heard a series of pops. Glancing in my rear-view mirror, I see the car behind me swerve, but I have no chance to react before I hear more pops and realize it's gunfire. The back end of my car swerves out as I struggle to control it. Twisting the wheel this way and that to control the skid, I have no choice but to break, even though fear practically paralyzes me.

Theo begins to cry as the car comes to a skidding halt on the side of the road. I instantly jump out of the car and run to my son, unclipping him and holding him tight to me, my hands all over him checking for any injury. Looking around I see the car with the guards some ways behind me.

Then in horror I watched as they get out only to be shot as their feet touch the concrete. Blood pools as their limp bodies hit the ground. Fear rises in my belly as bile hits my throat. I go to turn to run back to my car when a hand grabs hold of my hair from behind. The scream freezes in my throat at the sound of my ex-husband's voice.

"Where do you think you're running off to?" he says as he whips me around pushing me against the car. He looks so different, his hair is longer, his limp is almost gone. He looks strong and his eyes on me look cold. Stubble covers his jaw, the denim jacket he is wearing barely hides the gun that is strapped under his arm.

"I...I wasn't running," I stammer not knowing what to do but knowing I need to keep things calm.

"Oh Lexi, Lexi, still the little liar aren't we," he says as he runs a finger down my face. Where once his touch made me ripple with desire now it makes me shiver with fear. Theo begins to fuss, and Dean's attention drops to him, terror holds me in its grip when he reaches for my son. I shy away, turning so that my son is away from the stranger in front of me.

"I only want to see him, Lexi," Dean says with hurt in his voice. "You don't honestly think I would hurt an innocent baby, do you?" he asks.

I remain silent not knowing what to say. I try and look for a way out, knowing that if Dean gets me away from here then I'm dead. I decide to appeal to whatever sense of normal that might exist in his mind. "I think he might need to eat," I murmur.

Dean looks at me funny, a tilt of his head as if he is trying to figure me out. Then as if a light goes on he snaps out of it. "Of course, I have everything we will need in my van. You'll see, Lex. I've thought of everything." He is tugging my arm toward a blue transit van that is parked down the way in the layby. What does he mean, he has everything we will need?

"No, I need to go. Hunter will be worried," I say. Instantly I know it was the wrong thing to say.

His face darkens, his jaw starts to tic. "Hunter doesn't want you, I told you that. Why don't you ever listen to me, Lexi?" he asks as he pulls me harder making me fall to my knees. Gravel bites into me cutting the skin. He pulls me up and I take my chance. I kick him in the side of his knee and hear the scream as his leg buckles. I don't stay to see him fall, as soon as he releases me, I run toward the wooded area that runs along the road parallel to the river. I hold Theo to me and run as fast as I can. I can hear Dean roar behind me and pick up my speed. I know that if he catches me, he will kill me. I see it in his eyes that he is unhinged.

I duck into the densely wooded area letting the trees camouflage me, praying that the noise I'm making is drowned out by the sounds of him rushing through the woods.

"Come on, Lexi, don't make me chase you. Gracie did that, and I had to teach her a lesson." *Oh God what did he do to Grace, was that why she came to my house?* I stay still as I hide on the bank of the river, the noise masking my sounds even more, even though my heart is beating so hard I'm sure he can hear me. I look to my son as he starts to fuss, and I feel impotent tears hit the back of my throat. I hear Dean go past and hold my breath, wondering how long to leave it before I try to get to my car. I wait a few minutes before peeking out through the dense greenery.

I take two steps before I feel pain like no other shoot through my head as I'm hit from behind by something heavy. My knees buckle, and I fall, my vision blurs, blackness teetering on the edges of my vision. I hold tight to my son as Dean stands in front of me. His face weaves in and out of my sight as if he is dancing some sick hoola dance. He steps toward me as I try in vain to stay conscious. I see his arms come out as I fall sideways, and he pries my son from my arms as I scream and try to fight him, but I'm losing. My vision is fading.

His booted foot kicks me hard and I double over on my side as he holds my crying son.

"You shouldn't have fought me, Lexi. Grace fought me and now she is dead. Why do women lie and betray me?" He speaks to my son then as I cry, lying at his feet, unable to get my limbs to move as I go in and out of consciousness. "You won't betray me will you, son?" he croons, and I pull myself up with what is left of my energy to try and fight for my son. I crawl on hands and knees to him, blood running down my neck from the gash in the back of my head, my hands cut from the forest floor. Pain screams from my ribs where he kicked me, every breath hurts like a knife.

"Please," I beg as I grasp his leg. His hand strokes my cheek and he looks at me with such love that for a second, I feel hope that he feels regret and that I got through to him.

"I loved you, Lexi, Grace tricked me. But it was you I love., Then you betrayed me, you cheated on me, so I can't spare you. But I can't kill you. I'll tell you what, I'm going to give you a chance. I will leave you here and if you survive then so be it, if not then..." He doesn't finish his sentence, but shrugs. As if my living is up to fate.

He uses his foot to shove me down, kicking me toward the river until I land in the cold water. It is an instant shock and I suck in a breath as he holds me under until I feel my vision go white and my lungs burn with the need to breathe. My arms flay as I fight him and just when I feel I'm going to pass out he lets me up. The current pulls at me as I grab for the bank and miss. I watch as Dean walks away with my son in his arms as my body is pulled in the opposite direction by the force of the river. Hopelessness and grief overtake me as blackness pulls me under. My last prayer is that Hunter finds our son before it is too late.

CHAPTER TWENTY-TWO

HUNTER

MY LIVING ROOM LOOKS LIKE MISSION CONTROL, THERE
are computers and surveillance tech set up all over the
place. Jack and his men are looking at maps and tracking
Lexi and Theo's last known movements. I hate it. I hate it
all. Why didn't I pick up the phone when she called? Even
with all the money and power I have, I still couldn't keep
her and Theo safe.

A knock comes and I rush to the open the door,
hoping that maybe it's Lexi and there has been some
horrible misunderstanding. My hope is shot when my
parents look at me with shock and worry evident on their
faces. My parents seem to have aged since I saw them last,
fear and pain etched into every line.

"Hunter. My boy." My mother pulls me to her and
despite her treating me like a child I let her. I need the
comfort that only a mother can bring if only for a split
second.

"Mom," I say as I pull back.

My father squeezes my shoulder and I nod, not able to muster anything else. I have never felt more helpless and inept in my life.

"What can we do?" my mom asks.

Despite the horror of the situation I'm in, I feel an immense amount of love for my parents at that moment.

"I'm not sure, make some coffee maybe?"

She palms my cheek and looks into my eyes, eyes the same as hers and with conviction she replies. "We will find them, Hunter."

I nod because I don't know what else to say. The alternative is incomprehensible to me. I move over to Jack as he motions for me to join them.

"Mac, this is Alex, Reid, and Decker." He introduces the three other men.

Alex is tall, tan and should probably be modeling. Reid is covered from his neck to his knuckles in tattoos, with slicked-back, long hair and a biker vibe going on and Decker is tall, dark with the poshest British accent I have ever heard. Jack assures me they are the best and that is good enough for me.

It has been fifteen minutes since they'd arrived and set all their gear in my living room, turning it from a cool living space into a hive of activity. I'm looking to them to fix this shit storm because I'm out of my depth.

"Good to meet you," I say with a short nod.

"Reid is our hostage and extraction expert. We believe Dean has taken them somewhere from the preliminary profile Decker has done."

"Dean feeds off admiration and control. He still believes he can force Lexi into the perfect life he sees for them. We know that from the picture he sent her. We don't think Theo is in immediate danger and Lexi will be fine as long as she toes the line. The problem with people with this condition is that they are highly unstable and difficult to predict. It is of utmost importance for us to locate and extract them. That's where Reid comes in," Decker says as he unfolds his arms and points at Reid.

"Once we have them I'll formulate an extraction plan. It might need to be quick and we can't guarantee he will come out of it alive, but we will do our best."

"Do we have any news?"

Jack looks at Alex and I see something pass between them.

"Fucking tell me," I growl as I grab Jack by the collar and shove him.

Jack holds up his hands not attempting to defend himself. "Settle down, Hunter. We have an update, but you need to cool your shit. You're no good to anyone if you don't."

I let go and run my hands through my hair in frustration.

"We got word through a contact that the two men you hired have been found dead in the woods close to the road where the two cars were found. They were killed with single shots to the head. It was quick."

"Fuck," I spit as I feel nausea crawl up my throat. "What else do we have?" I need to calm down and help these men find my son and my woman. Being an emotional dick won't help anyone. There will be plenty of time to fall apart when they are safe.

"From what we can see, Dean has taken them. The car seat is missing and there are no signs of a struggle, but we have men sweeping the woods for any clues we might have missed. There are no traffic cams in that area but there is a big gap from when we lost them on one camera and pick him up on the next." He moves closer to the computer and hits some keys pulling up an image. I move in beside him, peering closer to try and see what he is trying to show me.

"If you look here you can see this van which has been registered under a fake identity. It moves down this road at eleven thirty-three and we pick it back up on this one," he points to the second screen, "at twelve forty-two. That is one hour and nine minutes longer than it should take to just snatch someone. We need to figure out what happened in that space of time. It is crucial to find out what happened."

"What about the van? Surely we can trace them through the traffic cameras and find out where he is?" I feel hope burn in my chest as Jack nods, but his face remains impassive.

"Yes, in theory, we can. We have Will tracking that now, but we suspect he will dump the van, so don't get your hopes up. We do have some other things up our sleeve. Don't worry Hunter, we'll get them back." Jack slaps me on the shoulder and then turns back to his men.

I'm summarily dismissed. I have to let go and let the people whose job it is, find Theo and Lexi. All I can do is wait.

CHAPTER TWENTY-THREE

LEXI

I'M SO COLD, SHIVERS OF ICE RUN THROUGH MY BLOOD AS water laps at my neck. Pain lances through every part of my body. I struggle to open my eyes, fighting through the fog of pain and nausea. *Theo, I must get to Theo.*

Opening first one eye and then the other I see that it is growing dark. How long have I been here and where exactly am I? The area looks so different from the place on the bank of the river where Dean pushed me in.

The feel of cold water against my skin makes me shiver which sends pain through me. I hear a noise and know it might be my only chance. I need to get help. I need to find Theo. Hunter will be so worried. My eyes sting with tears at the thought of Hunter terrified for us.

Hearing the distant sound again, I force my pain-wracked body to move. I reach for the tree root, grasping it with numb hands, my palms slip and I cry out in anguish. I have to get out of here or I will not survive the night. Even in this fog, I realize that in this condition and with the injuries I have, I'm going to be in trouble if I'm not found soon.

My head slumps and my body sags with exertion as I half pull myself from the water. I hear the noise again and then what sounds like a dog barking. I close my eyes determined to rest for just a second as my vision swirls.

A tongue licks my face and I startle awake. It is darker now, the sun hidden completely by the trees overhead. I look up to see a Cocker Spaniel dog lying beside me, its tongue lolling as it barks. It does not move away but licks my face again. I find it reassuring. The brown and white fur is soft as it touches my face.

I'm moving in and out of consciousness, when I hear distant voices. I need to tell them I'm here.

"We need to get her out of here, she's in a bad way."

I wonder who the poor person is they are talking about. I hope they can help her. I'm sleeping on a cloud nothingness, my pain receding far away. I'm light as a bird, but something nags at me. I need to remember something. I need to speak, to tell them, but I can't remember what it is.

Blackness is pulling at me as I fight it. I feel movement as if I'm being carried.

"Lexi, can you hear me?"

I try to answer but my words won't come.

"We're taking you UC hospital, Lexi. Just stay with us."

I want to tell them about Theo, ask them if they have found him. Panic hits me and I feel my chest start to tighten so I can't breathe. My lungs are bursting as I fight, my heart is beating too fast. There's a piercing sound of alarms in my ears as I feel blackness descend.

"Paddles, we're losing her!" I hear someone call out before my hearing goes and I'm floating on a sea of cotton wool. I like it here, there's no pain, no anger, but also no Theo and no Hunter. I need to go back. But I'm lost, I don't know which way to go. Light is pulling me one way and darkness the other. I stand at the crossroads and look for directions but there are none. I'm on my own.

CHAPTER TWENTY-FOUR

HUNTER

THE CALL COMES AT EIGHT THIRTY-FOUR THAT NIGHT. The day has been the longest and most arduous of my life. Pacing the condo, drinking coffee, and searching for any tiny clue in my brain for where he might have taken them. Has she mentioned anything in passing?

Jake and Cherry arrived not long after my parents. Cherry is visibly upset by her best friend going missing. I could see by the terror in her eyes that she thought he would hurt Lexi. I try to hold tight to the thought that he won't but in my gut, I know something is wrong. I feel it the same as if it were me.

Cherry is a fireball though, she marched up to Jack and demanded he tell her what she could do to help. Had it been any other situation it would have been funny to watch the five foot nothing pink haired warrior.

Jack told her to go to Lexi's place, which had been cleared and see if they could find any clue in her paperwork that might say were Dean had taken them. Jake has gone with her, saying he didn't think it wise she was left alone. Jack and Decker agreed that it was wise as Dean would use anything he could against Lexi to make her do as he wanted.

Sitting on our bed, which is still mussed from this morning, I take the nightshirt she'd worn in my hands, bringing it to my nose. I inhale the scent of her, it comforts me at once, yet at the same time it tears a hole in my chest from the pain of knowing he has them. How did this happen? I'd hired the best I could find, other than Jack's team, and still, I couldn't keep her safe. Maybe I should have made her stay in the condo, stipulated she was not to go out alone.

But I know my Lexi and she would have wilted. She would have resented me and the restrictions I had put on her. Lexi was like a flower that needed the people she loved to thrive. Keeping her away from them would have been allowing Dean to win.

I rub the fabric in my fingers, trying to draw strength from it. A noise at the doorway draws my eyes up and I see Jack standing there. His face is impassive, not an emotion evident on the man, everything is locked down, but I know. I can sense it.

"Tell me," I say as I stand, moving toward him.

"They found her."

Relief makes me miss a step, the feeling washing through me like a tsunami. "And Theo?" I ask as a new fear grips me hard.

"I'm sorry, Mac. They found Lexi by the river. She's is in a bad way. They are airlifting her to UC. There was no sign of Theo."

My knees buckle, and I almost go down but resolve to be there for her no matter what strengthens me.

"I need to see her," I say to Jack as I follow him out.

He does not try to console me or offer me false words of hope. He is precise and controlled dealing only in fact. It is what I need right now.

This is something I can do. I can be there for Lexi, help her deal with whatever that sick bastard has done to her. I feel useful for the first time since this shit started.

"Alex will drive you there now so you can be with her. But Mac, she is in a bad way, you need to be prepared."

I dismiss his words, not prepared to accept that she won't pull through, because it is abhorrent to me that she won't make it. "Just get me to her and find my son." I stride from the room, straight for the door where Alex is waiting with my parents.

"We will follow you, Hunter," my mom says. Her eyes are red-rimmed, but I can't offer her comfort, I'm barely holding it together now and need every atom of strength I have for my Lexi.

There is silence in the car. I'm lost in thought, worry about what he may have done to her making me feel sick with fury. We pull up outside the hospital and I'm out of the door striding for the door to the emergency room.

The nurse on the desk looks up as I enter. "Can I help you?"

"Lexi Crane, my girlfriend, has been brought in," I say hating the sound of his name on my lips. She looks down and begins typing. I fight the impatient need to shove her out of the way and just run through the emergency department looking for her. My hands clenched by my sides as I feel my parents come to stand at my back. My father's hand on my shoulder is like a calming balm, keeping me grounded.

"Take a seat and I'll page the doctor taking care of her."

I curb the urge to scream, to bellow out my frustration at not being able to see her immediately. Waiting is not a concept I'm used to, especially in this situation.

We take a seat on the blue plastic chairs, and the memory of Lexi calling them torture devices springs into my head. It is followed by a litany of memories—they play out like a movie in my mind. Lexi as she baked a cake for Theo's one-month birthday. Lexi as she laughed at the way I sang to my son declaring I had a horrible singing voice and would scare him. Lexi nursing Theo for the first time, exhausted from his birth, face red and looking more beautiful than I could put into words.

It feels like every moment together is etched like gold into my mind and I pray harder than I have ever prayed that this is not all I have left of her. My parents sit on either side of me, bolstering me with their strength and not for the first time today, I feel thankful to have them in my life.

It feels like interminable hours but in reality, it's only twenty minutes since I arrived when the doctor walks in, he is wearing scrubs and a mask is hanging around his neck.

"Mr. McKenzie?"

"Yes," I stand, walking toward him, so glad that Lexi changed me to her next of kin in the absence of her parents. The last thing I need now is a battle for information.

"Let's take a seat." He motions for me to sit.

"How is she?" I ask, half of me terrified of the answer, the other half desperate to know.

"Lexi is in a very poor state. She had a fracture to the

back of her skull, two broken ribs, and her spleen has ruptured. We are taking her into surgery now to remove her spleen. Luckily for her, the spleen did not rupture on impact but from the pressure of a small bleed inside the splenic capsule. The skull fracture looks to be a simple linear fracture, but we will monitor her very closely. She also has cuts and bruises on her hands and face. It looks like she put up quite the fight. She also has some signs of hypothermia from being in the river so long. We will keep you updated." He taps my shoulder and moves away down the hall.

Shock at the seriousness of her injuries keeps me from saying a lot. I mumble a thank you and sit with my head in hands. I have never felt fear like this, never understood bloodlust until this minute. I want to kill Dean, slowly and painfully. Make him hurt for all the pain he has caused her.

Cherry and Jake arrive and she comes over to me and wraps her arms around me, hugging me as if she needs it as much as I do. We cling to each other, our love for Lexi pouring from us.

"Any news?" she asks, her eyes rimmed with red. I can see she has been crying. Jake is at her back, his hand hovering as if he wants to offer her comfort but is unsure if he should.

"The Doctor came out about half hour ago." I tell her the list of injuries, watching as Cherry flaps her hand behind her looking for Jake. Her other hand comes to her mouth as she pales.

"What about Theo?"

Pain clutches me as I think of my son in the clutches of that madman. "Nothing. Jack and his team are working on it."

Cherry nods and sits beside my mother. They link arms silently.

"What can I do Mac?" my oldest friend asks.

I shake my head. "Nothing we can do. Did you find anything at the house?"

"Hard to say. We gave everything we had to Alex," Jake says as he points to the stoic man standing guard by the door, with a phone to his ear as he watches us closely. He looks like he should grace the covers of Vogue until you hear him speak and get close enough to see the cool intelligence behind his eyes. It is then that you can see he has seen things that have changed the core of him as a man. He is not the sum of his looks.

"Thank you."

We sit, each of us silent in our own thoughts. Mine are torn between worry for Lexi and worry for Theo. I pace the small waiting room, anxiety making me antsy. I hate not knowing what to do, not being able to help.

I cross to Alex who has just ended another call with Jack I presume. "Any news on Theo?"

"We have a lead that Reid and Decker are checking out now. The paperwork from Lexi's old home shows a sale agreement for a small plot of land out by Goose Creek Maysville. Has she ever mentioned it?"

I rack my brain for any familiarity with that name, but nothing comes up. "No, never."

"Well, we're going to check it out. As it was in his birth mothers name, there is a good chance that he would use it."

"Keep me updated."

"Will do."

I feel torn now. I want to stay and wait for news on Lexi—I need to see for myself that she is okay—but I know in my heart she would want me looking for Theo. Her mothering instinct would want me looking for our son.

I turn back to Alex who is regarding me silently, it's as if he knows what I'm going to say. "If you get confirmation he is there, I want to be there when you go and bring my son out."

Alex is taller than me, stronger than me, and considerably more trained than me. He could probably beat me to a pulp, controlled aggression seems to permeate from him. But I know in that second that if he says no, I will not think twice about going against him, no matter how much I respect him.

"Of course, I wouldn't expect anything different."

Relief that I have one less battle to fight fills me. I relay the information to my parents, Cherry, Jake, Darla, and Frankie who'd arrived about ten minutes earlier.

It is an hour later when the doctor walks out, his face showing signs of fatigue. I stand and as one we move toward him.

"Lexi made it through surgery. The next twenty-four hours are crucial. She still has the very real danger of her body going into shock. She lost a lot of blood and had to have a transfusion. But for now, she is stable."

"Can I see her?"

"Yes, one at a time though and give us a few minutes to get her settled."

"Thank you," I say as I shake his hand. My throat is clogged with unshed tears.

"You're welcome. The nurse will take you up in a few moments. She has a long recovery ahead, but she is strong. She wouldn't have survived otherwise."

I let out a shaky breath as I sit down heavily on the

chair. I'm beat, my emotions a shot but I have to summon up the strength I need for Lexi.

A few minutes later a nurse in scrubs calls my name. I follow her silently down the corridor to the intensive care ward. She opens a door and I hesitate, taking a second to muster my resolve before I enter.

She is lying in the middle of the bed, a white sheet pulled up to her chest, a hospital gown covering her. White bandages cover her, a stark contrast to the pale almost black bruises on her cheek, cuts, and grazes on her arms. She has a bandage on her head, a drip in her arm and an oxygen mask on her face. Machines are hooked up to her, beeping as they take readings of her heart and pulse.

"Don't be alarmed. The monitors are for us to keep a close eye on her, that's all."

I'm startled when the nurse speaks, it prompts me to move closer, seating myself beside her. I take her hand in mine, and it is soft and warm. She looks so incredibly sick and it petrifies me how close I've come to losing her. I kiss her palm as I bring it to my face, needing the physical contact to remind me she is okay.

"Is she in pain?"

"No, she is heavily drugged. The doctor is concerned about how she will react when she wakes and finds her baby still missing, so we are keeping her sedated to give her body a chance to heal. Talk to her though, she might be able to hear you."

The nurse bustles around quietly as I try to find words to say to Lexi. Never in my life have I struggled for words but now they escape me. How can I reassure her when I feel so lost myself? Then it comes to me.

CHAPTER TWENTY-FIVE

LEXI

I FIGHT THROUGH THE TUNNEL OF FOG TOWARD A SOUND that is familiar to me. I can't place it, but it seems like I should. It sounds like someone singing—badly. It is out of tune, but the sound gives me comfort as I try to place the voice and the words.

It is a lullaby, the words are sweet in the deep baritone voice. I want to reach out and touch it, but it seems so far away. I'm so tired, maybe I will just rest a bit longer. I let the words wash over me, bringing me a sense of peace and calm.

The sensation of someone touching my hand, stroking my face pulls me from the abyss where nothing can touch me. I float closer, feeling the touch and knowing that it is Hunter. His scent hits my nose and I struggle to open my eyes. I need to tell him something, a nagging feeling that something important happened and I need to tell him makes my heart race.

A profound feeling of desperation hits me as I battle to

open my heavy-lidded eyes. Hands on my arms and shoulders hold me as I fight to wake up. Loud beeping noises—alarms going off—filter through the haze in my head. *I have to tell him*. Theo! Dean has Theo. I have to tell Hunter. He has to save our son. The alarms are louder now, screaming in my head as I try to give voice to my thoughts. My heart feels like it is out of control.

Then a warm peaceful feeling hits me. My heart calms as heat runs through my veins, making me so sleepy. I can't remember what I wanted to say now. A kiss to my cheek feels nice and I curl up, warm in my black secluded mind where pain and desperation cannot touch me.

I hear a man sob and feel sorry for him. I want to offer comfort, but I'm too sleepy. He is drifting further and further away now as I fall into blessed unconsciousness.

CHAPTER TWENTY-SIX

DEAN

I GLANCE TO THE WHITE WICKER BASSINET IN THE corner of the cabin, my skin is itching. It feels like my skin is crawling with tiny bugs. I need to take a shower and wipe Lexi's blood off me. It is only a tiny speck, but it feels as if it is burning into my skin. Her eyes pleading with me to help her nearly broke my resolve, but I could see she didn't mean it. She would betray me the first chance she got.

I punch the wall of the log cabin—wood splinters and my knuckles sting with the force of the blow. I am angry that she tricked me again. I was weak, I should have killed her when I had the chance. But she wove her spell around me as she has always done. I flex my sore hand trying to stop the ache. If I had killed her, ended her life, she would be with my Grace now. My two perfect girls together, waiting for me, their King.

The baby cries, startling me from my thoughts. I

approach the crib where he is lying. His face is all scrunched up as if he is angry with the world—little arms and legs flying wildly. Reaching out slowly I stroke his tiny arm, he is so fragile, so innocent. Lexi should never have dragged an innocent baby into this. I startle sharply when the tiny human grabs my finger and holds on tight.

His dark brown eyes look at me as he tries to wrestle my finger to his mouth searching for food. A tug in my chest almost doubles me over. I feel a sense of completeness as this baby, my baby now, looks to me for his most basic human needs. I am the only one who can give him the food he desperately wants. It is a heady feeling.

"You hungry, Buster?" I ask him, using the name I have chosen for him. I chuckle to myself when he pulls my finger to his mouth, searching. Pulling away I move to the tiny kitchenette on the opposite side of the room. The formula and other supplies that I had stashed there three weeks ago are ready. I have been preparing for this since I found out Lexi was now living with *him*.

Hunter McKenzie! He is the man that ruined my life. He took what was mine. She was *my* wife, he had no right. I hope he feels every second of the pain I did when Lexi dies knowing he couldn't protect her. He tried to beat me, he lost, they always try to beat me, and they always lose. I am unstoppable.

My stomach hurts at the thought of her death, but it's her own fault. I tried to warn her, I tried to tell her, but she wouldn't listen. My Grace was the same. She tried to leave and when I told her how I had saved her, she wouldn't listen to me. She was not grateful for everything I did for her, she disrespected me. She ran, she pushed me until I had to teach her a lesson. She cried and begged me not to hurt her, great big tears running down her pretty cheeks even as I explained to her that I was releasing her from her pain, the tears still came. The peace in her eyes as I watched the life drain from her had been the most beautiful thing I had ever seen.

I had fallen in love with her even more at that moment, but I couldn't do that for Lexi. A cry from the corner reminds me that I need to feed the baby. Maybe when he is asleep I will go out and look for Lexi and finish what I should have earlier.

I cross to the fridge and fill the sterilized bottle with the formula, before warming it in a pan of hot water. Testing it on my wrist I decide it is the perfect temperature.

"Don't worry little guy, I have your dinner," I say as I lift him into my arms, a feeling of greatness filling me. I pop the nipple into his mouth. Instantly he starts to push the bottle away.

"Come on," I coax as he starts to fuss.

This is her fault, she knew I didn't like the idea of breastfeeding him. She has always been selfish. Eventually, he takes a few sucks and I manage to get a few ounces of formula down him. I burp him and change his diaper before settling him back to sleep.

I glance at the window, it is late afternoon now and I am not stupid. I know they will be coming. Moving to the back of my van I take out everything I need.

They think they can creep up on me, but I am ready for them. I am smarter than all of them. I always have been. Lexi stopped appreciating me though and that's why she has to be punished. Maybe leaving her alive is for the best. That way she will suffer the eternal punishment of knowing she couldn't protect her son, that she lost him. They lost and I am the victor.

I spend the next few hours setting up the tripwires and explosives. I lift the vest over my head and strap the remote to my belt buckle. When the time is right I will attach Buster to his carrier and fix him to my front behind the bomb. They won't dare to cross me or stop me then. I know Lexi and that weak-ass Hunter. They will do anything to save their son and I'm counting on it getting me of here and to safety.

I make myself a quick supper of noodles. They are watery and tasteless, but they will do for now. When I move on I will find a small town with a decent restaurant. Maybe Louisiana or New Orleans. The world is my oyster, well mine and Busters.

It is late and I feel tiredness pulling at me so I slip the vest on determined not to be caught off guard by anyone. I walk to the tiny crib and look down at the tiny, sleeping child. He is so peaceful, my chest feels heavy with thoughts of what could have been. Lexi and I could have raised him as our own, we would have been happy together as a family.

I decide to let him sleep. Lifting the crib I move it into the cooler bedroom with me, worried that he will get too hot as the air in the cabin is stifling. I place the crib on the other side of the bed and open the window the tiniest bit, making sure it is safe from any critters.

I move back to the living room and sit at the tiny table, laying out all the pictures I have taken of Lexi and Buster over the last few weeks. In some she looks so breathtakingly beautiful that I have to catch my breath to ease the tightness there. In some, she is looking at our son with such love and I know in those minutes she misses me. I can feel her love for me across the pixels of the image.

The silence outside suddenly makes me sit up straight. They are here, they have come for me. I stand and turn for the bedroom. It is time and they will not take my son from me.

CHAPTER TWENTY-SEVEN

HUNTER

"IF YOU CAN GIVE US A FEW MINUTES, MR. MCKENZIE," the nurse asks as they try to settle Lexi.

An hour after I had started to sing to her she started to come around as they reduced the amount of the drugs they have given her. As soon as she did, monitors had started to blare. Lexi started to thrash as if she was running from something or trying to say something.

I stand motionless as I watch the doctors and nurses try and calm her, eventually administering more drugs to put her back under.

"What the hell happened?" I ask as the doctor approaches me.

"We think Lexi was trying to come around and as the brain tries to process what has happened she was probably trying to communicate that, but the trauma to her body and mind means that any anxiety or stress puts her already weakened body under duress.

"She will be out for most of the day now, we had hoped

to bring her around, but we will leave her until later this evening before we try again."

I nod in understanding, pain in my heart for the fear I know she is feeling, I feel it too. The door behind me opens and my dad puts his head through. I beckon him in and he stares at the bed, his jaw ridged with anger.

"How is she?"

I realize that I haven't been out to update them. In my need to be with Lexi, I'd forgot that others care about her too.

"They are keeping her sedated. They tried to bring her around and she stressed out, so they think it best to keep her sedated for a while longer."

He nods as he pats the bottom of her foot. It is a simple gesture, but it touches me deeply. My family has come to love Lexi over the last few months.

"I need to speak with Alex. Will you stay with her? I know she is out, but I hate the thought of her being alone."

"Of course," he says as he takes a seat beside her.

When I walk out to the waiting room, I see Cherry is on the phone, my mother, Darla, Frank, and Jake are chatting quietly. My mother stands as I head over to her.

"Dad is going to sit with her. You can go in if you want."

"I'll let Cherry go in, that girl is worried sick over her friend."

I nod as I look to Cherry.

"I just got off the phone with Lexi's mom. They are booked on the eleven o'clock flight tonight."

It is only then that I realize the time. It has been nearly twelve hours since my son went missing. I wonder if he is hungry? He didn't like taking a bottle, he is a breastfed baby, preferring the comfort he receives from his mother.

"Alex do we have an update?" I ask as I approach him.

"Reid and Decker are due to check in any minute now," he says as his cell rings. He holds his finger up and steps slightly away, his head bowed. Undeterred I follow. If this is about Theo I want to know. I listen intently trying to read him as he nods and offers several yeses and nos.

Finally, he looks up and meets my eyes. A spark of something is there, the thrill of the chase maybe. He hangs up the call and speaks. "We have a positive ID on Dean and Theo. It seems he has a cabin on the land at Goose Creek. We have more men coming in for this extraction as it's going to be tricky."

"Why?' I ask not sure I want the answer.

"Dean has set up tripwires and explosives around the perimeter."

My stomach plummets and nausea shoots up my belly. I stagger fighting the burn of acid as it rushes up my stomach. Before I know what has happened I'm outside, pulling in deep lungsful of air. A hand on my neck is forcing me to bend so that my head is down.

"Just breathe, that's it."

I listen and take the oxygen in like I'm told. I stand, leaning back against the wall as I catch myself. Alex is watching me, hands on his hips, a calmness in his face. He has done this before, a million times and yet I sense that it is not just a job for him.

"I'm okay," I manage knowing I need to hold my shit together. My son needs me, and I won't let him down.

He nods and moves away. "I'll get the car, go tell your family what is happening."

It is a command and as much as it grates to be

commanded by anyone, this man and the Eidolon team are the only ones who can save my son. I text Jake who meets me at the door, I can't face seeing them all now and having my mother fuss.

Jake comes out a few moments later. "What's going on?"

"I need you to look after Lexi for me."

He looks perplexed. "Why? Where will you be?"

"They found Dean and he has Theo. I need to go with them. I need to be there for my son, but I can't do that unless I know Lexi has someone watching her back." I grasp his shoulder tight. "Do this for me, Jake. Please?"

"Of course, Mac. I won't let anyone near her except us and I'll make sure she isn't left alone. Go get your son and fucking end this once and for all." He is resolute as he looks me in the eye and I remember why he is my best friend.

I look toward the hospital once again torn between going to my son and staying with the woman I love, but I know she would want me to go, so I do. I turn my back on weakness and straighten my spine.

When we arrive, our position is three miles away from Dean's location. I was briefed by Alex on the way here. My job is to be there to observe, to take care of my son—along with a man named Waggs, who is their medic. We get out the vehicle and move toward the group of men. They are all dressed in black, including tactical vests, knives, and firearms strapped to them, it's unnerving, and I would hate to be on the wrong side of these guy's. They eye me as I move in beside Jack.

They are a solid unit, their eyes are not friendly, but they are not hostile, merely knowing.

"Mac, I want you to meet Waggs and Liam. Liam is our

demolition and explosives expert, he will be the one taking care of the tripwires and explosives that have been set up."

I shake the hand of the man with the short military haircut, his blue eyes are solemn as he nods at me. "Sorry it's under these circumstances mate," he says in a broad cockney accent.

Another man steps forward and he is older, closer to forty I would say, with a square jaw and hardness that make the others look friendly. He eyes me as he offers his hand, his eyes are cold, ice blue, his blond hair short.

"This is Waggs, he's ex-Green Beret and one of the finest medics I have ever met. He will be looking after Theo and checking him over when he is out."

"Nice to meet you, Hunter," he says in a familiar accent.

My eyebrows raise at the sound. "Lexington?" I say.

He nods. "Born and bred."

"We have cameras set up around the outer perimeter and now that you're here we will be ready to go in soon." Jack outlines the plan and my part in it which is basically to stay back and watch. They make me put on a tac vest over my button down, a comms unit is placed in my ear, so I can hear.

We walk in absolute silence toward the outer edge of the wooded area and I see the cabin come into view. It is small and crude, one light is on in the front of the cabin. As we move in Jack holds his hand up in a fist. I stop as do the others as Liam gets to work on the first tripwire. He makes short work of it before we continue. When we are less than a half a mile out we stop again. The clear night is both good and bad—it means it's easier for Eidolon but will also give Dean more sight. As the men beside melt away into the night I watch the directions they move in and even though I see them go, I can't see any sign of them. Not a blade of grass moves, not a twig snaps. They're truly like the ghosts of their name.

I'm left with Decker beside me as he watches his teammates move through his night vision goggles. I feel itchy with the need to race in there and grab my son. My heart aches as I hear the sound of a baby crying. I take a step, not knowing what I will do, but feel a firm hand on my shoulder.

"You will only endanger him if you go in there," Decker says in his posh British accent. I know he is right, but I fight an internal battle as I listen to my son's cries.

Help is coming son, I say in my head over and over. I stare out into the night knowing that they will be coming up on the cabin any second. My heart is in my throat as I listen, waiting for hell to reign down on that sick bastard and praying so hard that my son is spared. I make so many deals with God asking that he spare my son. I even offer Him myself in exchange knowing that I would gladly die to save him.

Then I hear it—the pop of gunfire. The crying intensifies as shouts are heard and then the sound of an explosion fills the air and my heart explodes with pain as I fear the worst.

CHAPTER TWENTY-EIGHT

HUNTER

Ears ringing, I find myself running, moving toward the noise and smoke that fills the air. I shrug off the hand that reaches for me, my only goal is to get to my son. Shouts are coming from the area around the cabin as I race across the expanse of grass that separates me from Theo.

Smoke fills the air around me, dust and debris floating all around as I push away the terror that is racing through my veins. Uncertainty and pain battle to bring me down but I won't let them bury me.

I round the edge of the cabin heading for the door that is hanging off its hinges when I'm hit by a brick wall. Jack and Reid almost tackle me to the ground as they try and stop me from moving forward gripping me hard across the chest. I fight to free myself, landing a hit here and there not caring who I must go through to get to my son.

"Theo," I shout. The noise wrenched from me sounds like a plea. I fight the hands that restrain me, determined to get to my son. Nothing else is in my mind but protecting my son.

"For fuck's sake, Mac! Don't make me knock you out," Jack yells in my face as he tries to get my focus on him rather than the cabin that is now billowing with smoke.

"I need to get to Theo." I can feel anger and pure unadulterated terror for my son battling in my head.

"He's fine, Mac. Look!" He points behind me and I turn to see Waggs walking toward me. He's covered in dust, a tiny bundle cradled to his chest, his large hands covering most of his head and body. My heart stutters and then I'm on my feet racing toward my son. Waggs hands him to me and I cradle him to my chest tight, kissing his head, almost sagging to the ground with relief. For one terrifying minute, I'd thought the worst. I cannot even say the words in my head they are too terrible to conceive. I pull back to check him and he looks up at me blinking his big brown eyes, tears wet on his long dark eyelashes.

"Daddy's got you, Theo," I say, and I feel wet on my cheeks as my son shoves his fist in his mouth and whimpers.

"Let's get you away from this smoke so Waggs can check him over properly," Alex says as he motions back toward the vehicle and Decker who is glaring at me.

I'm reluctant to let my son go as we reach the truck, but I lay him down gently on a blanket that someone has placed there and step aside for Waggs to check him over, though I do not give him much space. I can't quite bring myself to let go of the tiny hand that is wrapped around my thumb.

With utmost gentleness Waggs feels Theo's legs and arms, palpating his tummy. I can't take my eyes off my son, waiting eagerly for Waggs assessment.

"He looks good to me, but we should get him checked by a pediatrician. He was quite close to the blast and his ears are very delicate. You're a tough guy aren't you, champ," he says with a grin at my son.

I lift my son to my arms, and hold him to me, wrapping my arms around him to keep him warm. Everything happens quickly then. Alex moves to the vehicle and speaks quietly to Waggs, before moving closer to me and jumping into the driver's seat.

"What happened?" I ask when Alex and I are en-route to the hospital.

He glances at me, his face guarded. "Dean is dead," he says without emotion. "He had some sort of explosive device attached to him. Waggs went in the back with Liam, while Reid, Jack, and I converged from the side and front. Theo was in the back room, so when Dean exploded the device he was out of the direct line."

I'm shocked at the turn of events, a thousand 'what if' scenarios running through my head at once. "Was anyone hurt?" I ask praying that nobody was.

Alex shakes his head. "No. The device was pretty basic, so the blast radius was small. Most of the guys managed to take cover but Reid was closest to the blast and I figure he'll have some ringing in his ears for a bit, but other than that they are fine. It was pretty routine in the end."

I shake my head, slightly amazed that anyone can think of this as routine. I stroke my finger over Theo's sleeping form as he sits in the car seat, his pudgy fist in his mouth. These guys literally think of everything.

I can't wait to reunite Theo with Lexi. I just need my family home and safe. I can't imagine ever wanting to let them out of my sight again.

Everything is a blur once we reach the hospital. Theo

is whisked away by the pediatric team. I hover beside them not prepared to be separated from him for even a second. I look up toward the door when I hear a commotion before the door swings open and my mother walks in. Her feisty, southern temper aimed at the nurse who is trying to bar her entry.

"Bless your heart, if you don't move I'm gonna skin your hide and nail it to the barn door." Her sweet smile does little to lessen the threat. The nurse huffs and blusters as she turns to our private doctor who is looking over Theo.

"It's fine, let her in. Vivian good to see you." He smiles as if his nurses being threatened by perfectly coiffed Southern Belles was the norm.

"I'll be better when you tell me my grandson is okay!" she replies as she kisses my cheek and peers at Theo.

Dr. Carter, who had been my childhood doctor, hands Theo back to me along with a special bottle that had been filled with formula.

"He's as healthy as a horse."

"What about his ears?" I ask as Theo wastes little time latching on to the bottle.

"His eardrums are intact so there is no damage. They are a little red, but I suspect that's from teething."

"Isn't it too early for teeth?"

Dr. Carter shrugs. "Maybe a little but some babies do start early."

"So, I can take him home?"

"Yes, but I would like to follow up in a few days just as a precaution," he says as he sees my face change back to one of worry.

"Thank you."

"Don't thank me. Whoever protected him from that

blast is the one you should thank". With that he nods at my mother and leaves the room.

I wonder if Alex is playing down what happened in that cabin, but then let it go. The main point is Dean is dead and Theo is safe.

My mother sits beside me as I feed Theo his bottle. She doesn't say a word, as if she senses I need this time. Then she quietly stands, kisses my head, and leaves the room. I offer her a smile, but I'm too overcome to speak. Instead, I just hold my son as he feeds himself into a milk induced sleep. Looking at him I thank God that he will have no memory of the past twenty-four hours.

While it will haunt me and Lexi until the day we die, my son will be none the wiser. That is the only saving grace in this horrendous nightmare. Closing my eyes for a just a second, I let relief flow through me, exhaustion tugging at me.

The next thing I know, Cassie is shaking my shoulder. "Hunter."

I sit up as she eases a sleeping Theo from my arms. I rub my hand over my face and look at the clock. I haven't been out long, barely twenty minutes.

"How are you doing?" Cassie asks.

I don't know how to answer that right now. I feel kind of numb. I'm beyond relieved that Theo is safe, furious that Dean took the easy way out and got away with everything he did to us, and terrified for Lexi.

"Honestly, Cass. I'm kind of numb."

"Just take some time to process everything."

"I need to see Lex. Has she come around at all?"

"No, but one of us was with her the entire time. Jake had to wrestle Cherry out of there." I smile a small smile at that. Cherry is a hand full so I'm sure she gave Jake shit. That I wish I had seen.

"Would you like me to watch Theo while you get some rest?"

I hesitate not wanting to let Theo out of my sight.

As if she senses my dilemma Cassie asks, "How about I see if we can get a private room and then I can watch Theo in there while you sit with Lexi?"

I reach for her hand, squeezing it in thanks. "That's great, thanks Cass."

"No problem," she replies.

She hands Theo back to me as he starts to cry. I rub his back gently in circles, not sure who I'm soothing. I watch as Cass walks to the door, grateful that I have my family and friends around me.

Hopefully we will all be back to a new normal in a few weeks' time.

CHAPTER TWENTY-NINE

LEXI

I lean back to survey myself in the mirror, I look good—I think. I have finally regained the weight I lost after my surgery and my face has lost its pale pallor. I run my hands down the short black lace dress, turning slightly to see if the back looks okay. Two tiny diamante buttons hold the dress at the top and then the back is cut out. It is low and daring, almost touching the base of my spine.

I'm happy with how it looks and excited for Hunter to see it. I really want to wow him tonight. He has been amazing, looking after both me and Theo as I heal. I want to show him how much I appreciate everything he has done.

I still feel a small amount of blame for what happened and think I always will. I can't believe Dean kept all he did from me. I guess I saw what I wanted to see. He was not the man I thought he was, but I still feel sadness even after everything he did. He was a huge part of my life and he never got the help he so desperately needed.

I push any thoughts of what happened away. It's in the past and I only have room in my life for the present and my future with Hunter and Theo. It hasn't been easy though and most nights I'm still plagued by nightmares, but I'm working with a therapist now, determined to put it behind me.

Tonight, it is exactly a year since I met Hunter at Jimmy's. We are going out to celebrate our anniversary. Both of us feel that our lives together started that night. Just because we weren't together physically doesn't mean anything, in our hearts we were.

I add a silver arm cuff and long silver earrings that almost skim my shoulders. My hair is down around my shoulders, but the signature blue has changed. It was time for something new, so I went for bright purple tips in my hair. It isn't the pink Cherry was trying to persuade me to get but she even admitted the purple tips look awesome.

Sitting on the bed to slip on my silver diamante strappy sandals, I hear Hunter reading to Theo. I smile as I listen to them. They are so cute together that it melts my heart, forcing a lightness that I could never have imagined possible. They have given me something I didn't know I was missing—acceptance and unconditional love.

I buckle the ankle strap and stand, walking to the dresser I spritz myself with Chanel Mademoiselle. The brochure there catches my eye and I can't help the smile that spreads across my face. I pick up the realtors brochure and look at the house we have just bought. I'd insisted on putting everything I'd made on my old house into this one. It is a six-bedroom property with lots of land for Theo to run around on. It also has a large pool, a small stable and paddock, and even a separate detached workspace for me. It is a colonial design we both love and best of all it's only ten minutes away from our family and friends but still gives us the privacy we are still looking for. It is my dream home and I fell in love the minute we walked in.

I want to feel as if I contribute to our partnership. I know Hunter makes more money than God, but I won't be a kept woman. I need my independence and he respected that—eventually. Hunter has been so careful with me since I came out of the hospital, but tonight I need to tell him that it stops. He doesn't need to treat me like I might break if he disagrees with me or if he makes love to me.

He hasn't touched me since my operation and I'm starting to wonder if he doesn't want me any longer, but after a chat with my mom and Cherry, I now think he's scared to hurt me. I need to show him that I won't break. He was hurt too, maybe not physically but what he went through mentally haunts him.

I see it when I catch him watching me—the fear and pain in his eyes. He'd gone through Theo's disappearance without me and then everything that came afterward, including my very slow recovery.

I twirl around as the door opens, wanting to see his reaction. His eyes find mine, heat flares in them before he takes a slow journey of discovery down my body with his eyes.

"Wow, you look stunning," he says as he comes closer.

I look up as he gets near, my hands instantly going to his chest. "Thank you," I say as his hands rest on my hips, pulling me flush to his hard body—his very hard body. Bending he sniffs my neck, inhaling deep. I feel the heat of his hands on me, his grip tightening as I wind my arms around his neck.

"You smell good enough to eat too," he growls into my neck. The reverberation runs through my body like an electric pulse. Tiny goosebumps pepper my skin and I shiver at the feel of him against me.

"I'm not stopping you," I whisper, using my tongue to flick the lobe of his ear. The groan of need that comes from his throat is heady. His palms cup my ass and he pulls me even closer until our bodies are one.

"You're going to be the death of me," he chuckles as he kisses my neck before releasing me. His eyes find mine, the swirling blue almost hypnotizing in its intensity. I see so many things in the look he is giving me—love, desire, need, fear. All of it is written in his eyes. I catch my breath at the knot in my chest. His hand comes up and cups my cheek, his fingers curling around the back of my neck, tunneling through my hair.

I lean into his hand, turning my face to kiss his open palm, as I cup his hand in my much smaller one.

"I love you, Pretty Girl," he says with strained emotion in his voice.

"I love you too, Hunter, so much."

He bends to kiss me, his lips a mere whisper as they hover over mine, his eyes close and he pours every ounce of feeling into a kiss that is so sweet, so passionate, and so heartbreakingly beautiful that I know I will remember it until I'm old and gray. He pulls back, dropping one last simple kiss on my lips.

Opening his eyes, he steps back putting space between us.

"Now let's go before I change my mind about us going out and make your sweet ass the entertainment. And you look too beautiful not to show off."

I grin and sway my hips playfully as I walk away. Turning to see the lecherous look on his face as he watches. "Come on, Mr. McKenzie, don't keep a girl waiting."

I squeal, giggling like a school girl, then move my ass as he chases me. Thankfully our son sleeps well, or we would not be going anywhere tonight.

Vivian and Hank are in the living room and I go over to hug and kiss them both. They have become like second parents to me and I love them both dearly. I can't help but think how lucky my son is to have such a big, loving family around him. My parents are tying up loose ends in Greece and moving back here permanently. It upset them too much to be away from me when I was sick.

So, they had a meeting with the other family members and sorted out a different care arrangement for my grandmother. She was now living in a sheltered village for older people and apparently loving it. It has given her a new lease on life, the facilities are second to none. It is a huge relief for my mom and dad.

"Shall we get going?" Hunter asks as he lays his hand at the small of my back. I feel a shiver go through me and the smug look in his eye told me he felt it too.

"Yes, of course, let me grab my jacket."

When I return, Hunter is giving his parents a list of what to do with Theo. I feel my lips quirk as his father rolls his eyes.

"We have done this before, Hunter," Vivian says with a laugh as she takes the list.

"I know, I know, I just.... Oh whatever," he says as he kisses his mother's cheek.

"Have fun." They wave as we step into the elevator.

WE ARE SEATED in the corner, a quiet corner of the exclusive French restaurant. Tiny candles are the only light in the room, pristine white tablecloths cover the tables with small elegant vases of white orchids on each table. It is the most romantic restaurant I have ever been too. The food is divine. Hunter and I have just finished our main course of grilled bream with mustard and tarragon sauce for me and duck breast with passion fruit sauce and crushed peppercorns for Hunter. That had followed a starter of scallops with apple salad. Now we were waiting for dessert, a violet and blueberry panna cotta with meringue.

Hunter fills my champagne flute with more Champagne. I'm about to ask what we are going to toast when the waitress arrives with our dessert. As she lays the plate down, Hunter stands and moves so he is beside me. I look up, my heart fluttering wildly in my chest as he drops to one knee. He opens a ring box to reveal the most beautiful marquise-cut diamond solitaire.

I can feel my eyes well with tears as my shaky hand comes to my mouth.

"Lexi, ever since the day our eyes met at the bar, you have held me captive with your beauty, your compassion, your drive, and your determination. I can't conceive of a better mother for our son and you are the absolute best part of me. You complete me in a way that I didn't even know was missing. I love you more with each breath I take. Will you do me the greatest honor of my life and become my wife, my partner, in every way?"

Tears are running freely down my face as a wobbly

smile splits my face. "Yes, one thousand times, yes," I say as I fall to my knees, flinging my arms around him, kissing him hard. He lifts us both twirling me around as he does, before sitting me back on my feet.

"You won't regret it, Lex," he says as he slips the diamond ring over my knuckle.

"I know I won't," I say softly.

We eat our dessert with massive grins on our faces as we discuss our future. A future littered only with happiness.

LATER THAT NIGHT as we sway to a slow song on the dance floor at Jimmy's we reminisce about the last time we were here.

"I knew the minute I saw you I was gone for you," Hunter says as he holds me close.

"Yeah?"

"Yeah, it felt like my heart already knew you. Some magnet was pulling us together and we were powerless to stop it."

"I felt the same. I remember I wanted to bitch slap the waitress that was flirting with you at the bar. I'd never felt like that before, then you looked at me and it was as if everyone else ceased to exist in my world."

"They did cease to exist in mine. You were mine from the second we spoke. I have never felt anything like it, and I still feel it now every time I look at you. I sometimes think I can't love you more and then you say something or do something and prove me wrong."

"Keep talking like that and you are so getting lucky tonight." I giggle like a school girl when he picks me up, tosses me over his shoulder, and walks for the exit.

"Time to go home." Hunter laughs, his deep baritone sending spikes of need down to my very core. *Oh yeah, he is getting very lucky tonight or maybe it's me that is lucky.*

CHAPTER THIRTY

LEXI

"I CAN'T BELIEVE YOU'RE GETTING MARRIED," CHERRY squeals as she helps me into my wedding gown.

"I know, who would have thought all those months ago that we would be here now?" I answer as I look at myself in the mirror. My gown is an ivory lace fit and flares with a train. My arms are bare, the neckline is high at the front with a low sheer net back. I fell in love with it on sight and can't wait for Hunter to see me in it.

"You look beautiful," my mom says as she and Vivian dab their eyes.

Mom and Vivi, as she has asked me to call her, have become close since my parents moved home nearly nine months ago. My dad and Hank too. I never thought when I met Hunter how much we could all gain, how a tiny child and our love for each other would form bonds that would last a lifetime.

"Thanks, Mom," I reply.

The necklace she gave me earlier is fastened around my

neck, a blue sapphire on a platinum pendant that was my grandmothers. Matching earrings hang from my ears. I'm wearing my hair up in a sleek twist, it is elegant and classy, the blue in the front adding my own unique twist. A long veil is attached at the back and a tiny crystal tiara completes my wedding ensemble.

I decided to go back to blue for today as it is the color I was when we met, and today is the culmination of that.

We are getting married in Hank and Vivian's home. The sun is shining, and the grounds look beautiful with flowers and greenery. We wanted an intimate wedding— this wasn't about anyone else but us and we only wanted our friends and family. I hadn't realized quite what a furor it would cause until we were approached by a magazine to cover our wedding. We turned it down instantly, not wanting the publicity. There had been enough stories written about Hunter and me.

I hear childish laughter, followed by deep masculine chuckles coming from the room below and a smile creases my face. Theo will be one tomorrow and has just found his feet. He is the apple of his father's eye and so much like Hunter, even down to the stubborn look they both get when they don't want to do something.

We decided to wait to get married, wanting all the past dealt with. My therapist had suggested I visit Dean's grave and tell him how he'd made me feel. Hunter stayed in the car while I visited the grave, and although I know it upset him deeply, he respected my decision.

I had cried and wailed at him and then finally cried for the man he could have been if the sick disease in his mind hadn't won. It had been cathartic, a release that had finally put the nightmares to bed. I have not had one since and truly feel as if it happened to someone else.

A knock on the door breaks me from my musings and I turn as my father walks in—the look on his face says it all. Love shines from his eyes and for the first time I see him free from the pain he felt when I was attacked and he wasn't here to help me. I'm his little girl and it had affected him deeply. Now all I see is love and pride.

He moves to me as Cherry, Vivian, and my mom leave us. I know Cherry will help Cassie with Mellie and Theo so that Hunter can get ready. Cassie and Mellie are my bridesmaid and flower girl respectively and Cherry is my maid of honor. Theo is our ring bearer and Jake is Hunters best man. The rift between the two men has healed. I wish I could say the same for Cherry and Jake.

Their dislike still runs deep, and it troubled me at first but then I realized that I can't control everything, and it's not up to me to decide their happiness. So now we ignore them when they snarl at each other.

Taking my hands my father kisses both of my cheeks. "You look so beautiful, my Alexis," he says, and I see tears form in his eyes.

"Thank you, Daddy," I say, taking a deep breath to control my emotions.

"I'm so glad you found a man that can love you for who you truly are. Now I can walk you down the aisle knowing that I'm giving you to a man who deserves you."

A lone tear slides down my face and I swipe it away with the back of my hand.

"Stop," I laugh trying to lighten the moment. "You're going to ruin my makeup and then Cherry will kill me." We both laugh at that. I bend to pick up my bouquet of ivory ranunculi, roses and baby's breath with eucalyptus and take my father's arm.

"Ready?"

"So ready," I reply with a smile.

I LOOK up as the violinist starts to play and my breath catches as butterflies abound with excitement in my tummy. Hunter looks dashing in a black tuxedo his eyes are fixed on me and so full of love. He smiles, and I feel my feet moving, taking me closer to him and our future.

When I'm standing next to him, my father gives him my hand and kisses my cheek.

"Look after her, she is precious," he says softly, and I feel my eyes tear up.

"I will, Sir. She is the most precious woman in the world to me."

We look into each other's eyes as the minister starts the ceremony. We speak our lines, then our vows to each other—it is a beautiful blur and then we are husband and wife.

"You may kiss the bride."

Hunter grins and it is full of promise and his lips touch mine in a soft kiss that turns passionate until we hear throats clearing. We pull away laughing and look to the crowd that is gathered, they are all grinning madly.

I feel a tug on my leg and look down to see my son using my dress to keep himself steady. He looks adorable in a baby tux, his dark hair combed into a semblance of a style.

"Hey, baby," I say as I reach down, but Hunter is there first, swooping down and lifting him into his arms so he is between us.

"You jealous daddy got kisses and you didn't buddy?" Hunter laughs.

I kiss his baby soft cheek breathing in the scent that is all Theo. It is hard to convey how incredibly lucky I feel to have Hunter and Theo—they are my life.

Theo pats my cheek with his pudgy hands.

"Are we ready, Mrs. McKenzie?" Hunter asks, echoing the question my dad asked me earlier. The love shining in his eyes is almost more than I can bear.

"Yes. Let the dancing commence, Mr. McKenzie,"

The day has been perfect. Laughter, family friends, great food, all surrounded by love. We have smashed plates much to Theo's delight, now it is time to throw the garter and the bouquet.

I stand with my back to the eager single ladies and then throw. Turning, I see Cherry has caught it and I smile as she glares at me.

"You did that on purpose," she states with a mock glare.

I poke out my tongue because I really did.

We stand beside each other, arms linked as Hunter prepares to throw the garter that he took off my thigh, in what should have a PG-rated move but had felt like a prelude to something much sexier. He throws the garter over his head and a whoop goes up as Jake catches it.

I feel Cherry squeeze my arm. "I'm going to kill you for this," she says out of the corner of her mouth.

I laugh knowing she doesn't mean it. "Just get to it," I say pushing her toward the middle of the dance floor.

Jake will now have to put the garter on her leg as she sits in the middle of the room, while we all watch.

Cherry is my best friend in the world and I know as she sits down and lets Jake do just that, with his teeth and a very sexy grin I might add, that there is more to come for the two of them. The electricity coming from them is enough to light all of Cincinnati.

"Dance with me?" Hunter asks as he holds his hand out.

"It would be my pleasure," I say as he sweeps me onto the dance floor for our first dance. It took weeks to find our song, but when we did, it said everything about us. Everything by Michael Bublé seems to fit what we feel for each other.

Hunters arms are loose around my hips, my body tight to his as my arms go around his neck.

"Happy?" he whispers as he nuzzles my ear with his nose.

"Happier than I have ever been. You?"

"I don't think I could be happier," he replies with a grin.

"I bet I can make you happier," I whisper in his ear, my voice low and seductive.

"You think so, Mrs. McKenzie?" he replies with a lecherous grin, as his hands begin to wander lower, until they rest on my ass.

"Get your mind out of the gutter." I say then laugh.

"But it's so much fun in the gutter with you there with me," he says as he presses into me, showing me exactly how low his thoughts have gone.

I reach up and whisper into his ear, my lips feathering over his as I feel his breath on my neck. He tenses at my words and then pulls back. His face is awash with wonder as his eyes drop to my flat stomach.

"Really?" he asks his voice full of awe.

"Yep, I did the test this morning. We're having a baby."

"We're having a baby," he says as he lays his hand against the place our child is growing. "When?"

"Well, it's very early days so I guess in around seven and a half months."

"So, around Valentine's day?"

"I guess."

He crushes me to him and then kisses me, it is passionate and full of promise. "When can I tell everyone?"

"When we have the scan. We don't want to jinx anything."

"Okay. God, Lex, you did it again."

"What?" I ask with a feeling of puzzlement.

"Every time I feel I can't love you more, you give me something else and I love you more."

"I love you too, Hunter. So much."

"How about we get out of here and I show you how much I love you?"

"Lead the way."

It is past midnight and Theo is spending the night with my mom and dad. We leave for our honeymoon late tomorrow—four glorious weeks in Europe. We will stay with Will Granger for a few days before heading back to London, then Paris, before finishing up in Italy.

Will and his brother Jack have become close friends after what they did for Hunter and me, which is why he was invited to the wedding. Neither could make it, but Waggs and Alex had been stateside and were able to attend. In my book, those men will always be classified as friends and Hunter has said as much.

Alex seems to be a big hit with the ladies in my family, but it's Waggs dancing with Cassie that catches my eye. *Um, now that was one to watch.* I nudge Hunter in the ribs as we walk toward Hank and Vivian to say goodnight.

"Look," I point with my chin, not wanting them to see.

Hunter's eyes follow mine and he smiles. "Um, well, he best behave himself, or Green Beret or not, I will kick his ass," he states.

"Hunter, behave. She's just having fun."

"Um," he says as he watches them. I love how protective he is of the women in his life. God help us if this little one is a daughter I think I as I touch my hand to my tummy and smile. Today has been perfect and I'm so glad we got to share it with the people we love. I can't wait to see what the future holds for us all.

EPILOGUE

HUNTER

As I carry Lexi over the threshold of our Hotel room, I feel a sense of coming full circle. This is the room where it all began.

"I can't believe you got this room," she says as she kisses my neck.

"It feels right," I say as I set her down on the bed.

"Yes, it does," she says. Her eyes are heavy with desire as they travel over me and my body burns for her. I wonder if it will always be this way and somehow, I know it will. Bending, I take her ankle in my hands kissing my way up her calf. I lick the back of her knee, nibbling lightly, the taste of her skin like nectar to me. I repeat the move on her other leg, leaving her strappy ivory heels on as I push the dress higher, so I can caress the soft skin of her thighs. Tonight is about worshiping her body, reaffirming our love. I reach down, pulling Lexi up so she is standing.

"Turn around." My voice is husky as she does what I

say without question. The trust she has humbles me. I have been dying to get this dress off her since I saw her in it. Luckily, the tiny buttons are mainly for show and hide a zipper that slides down easily. The dress catches on her hips, revealing the top of her lace G-string. Her back is bare, and my body hardens even more at the thought that she has been mostly naked underneath this dress all day.

As the dress slips to the ground, I take the time to admire the graceful curve of her back, the way her small waist nips in before her hips flare. Her ass is pure perfection. I ache to be inside her but resist the urge to rush this knowing that we will never get this night back.

I smooth my hand over the cheeks of her ass, and delight in the shiver that goes through her as she arches back into my touch.

"You like that, Pretty Girl?" I ask as I kiss her neck, palming her breasts, rubbing the tips with my thumb.

"Yes," she says on an exhale.

"Turn around, I want to see you." She turns, and I inhale sharply, she is so beautiful, her body turns me to stone from just the thought of it. "You're so beautiful, Lex," I say as I reach for her, pulling her close, kissing her until we are breathless and dizzy with need. Tongues dancing, lips melting together, in a rhythm as old as time.

I lay her on the bed and shed my clothes as she watches me, her arms braced on her elbows. Her tongue comes out to lick her full bottom lip and I groan. Stepping toward her I stand between her legs as she sits up, her heeled feet on the floor and she looks like every dirty dream I've ever had.

I hiss as she takes my cock in her hand, pumping it once, twice before she lowers her head. Her lips on my cock is pure unfettered heaven. She licks around the head before opening her mouth and looking up at me. Her mouth slowly descends, and I throw my head back, as I tunnel my hands into her hair, knocking the pins from her elegant twist. Her lips are swollen as she bobs her head up and down my cock.

It feels so good that I start to thrust into her mouth. I'm on the edge, but I don't want things to end this way. I reluctantly pull away and she frees my rock-hard cock with a pop.

"Lie back," I say as I push her shoulder gently, until she is lying back. I fall to my knees, sliding her panties down to reveal her to me. She is already wet for me, her need glistening of her thighs.

I lick a path from her knee to her center, tasting what I do to her on my tongue. She tastes so good, I'm sure I could get drunk on the taste of her. She moans as I kiss and lick my way over her lips before sucking her clit into my mouth. Her back arches from the bed as her hands grip my hair, showing me what she wants.

Her body peaks and she moans my name over and over as her climax rocks through her. I kiss her one final time before I rise up on my arms, hovering over her body. Her eyes are swirling with emotion, and she doesn't try to hide any of what she feels as I push into her. Her hands grip my biceps and as I feel her body tight around me. It is like coming home. A sense of completeness floods my body as she wraps her legs around me.

I start to slide in and out of her perfect heat trying to go slow as I kiss her neck, cupping her breasts as I swirl my tongue around the peak before sucking it into my mouth. Her moans and mewls fill my ears urging me on as she chases her release.

I feel the start of her climax as her body ripples around

me. It feels so good, I know I won't last much longer. Pressing my thumb to her clit I circle once and that's all it takes for her to climax.

My name is like a plea on her lips as she screams it over and over as her body milks my release from me. It is almost blinding in its intensity, our eyes locked on one-another—a connection so strong it will never be broken, not on this earth or where we go after.

Finally, I collapse beside her rolling her into my arms. She cuddles into me with her head on my chest as our breathing evens out.

"Thank you, Hunter," she says and I still the hand that had been stroking her bare shoulder.

"What for?"

"For finding me," she whispers. Her voice is not sad, but it is poignant.

"You're welcome. Thank you for loving me, Lex."

"Easiest thing I ever did," she replies as she looks at me.

I know our lives won't always be sunshine and rainbows, but I know that whatever test we are sent we will be okay because we have what most people spend a lifetime looking for—a true and perfect love.

BOOKS BY MADDIE WADE

FORTIS SECURITY

Healing Danger (Dane and Lauren)

Stolen Dreams (Nate and Skye)

Love Divided (Jace and Lucy)

Secret Redemption (Zack and Ava)

Broken Butterfly (Zin and Celeste)

Arctic Fire (Kanan and Roz)

Phoenix Rising (Daniel and Megan)

Nate & Skye Wedding Novella

Digital Desire (Will and Aubrey)

Paradise Ties: A Fortis Wedding Novella (Jace and Lucy & Dane and Lauren)

Wounded Hearts (Drew and Mara)

Scarred Sunrise (Smithy and Lizzie)

Zin and Celeste: A Fortis Family Christmas

Fortis Boxset 1 (Books 1-3)

Fortis Boxset 2 (Books 4-7.5

EIDOLON

Alex

Blake

Reid

Liam

Mitch

Gunner

Waggs

Jack

Lopez

Decker

ALLIANCE AGENCY SERIES (CO-WRITTEN WITH INDIA KELLS)

Deadly Alliance

Knight Watch

Hidden Obsession

Lethal Justice

Innocent Target

Power Play

RYOSHI DELTA (PART OF SUSAN STOKER'S POLICE AND FIRE: OPERATION ALPHA WORLD)

Condor's Vow

Sandstorm's Promise

Hawk's Honor

Omega's Oath

Lyric's Truth (coming soon)

SHADOW ELITE

Guarding Salvation

Innocent Salvation

Royal Salvation

Stolen Salvation

TIGHTROPE DUET

Tightrope One

Tightrope Two

ANGELS OF THE TRIAD

01 Sariel

OTHER WORLDS

Keeping Her Secrets *Suspenseful Seduction World* (Samantha A. Cole's World)

Finding English P*olice and Fire: Operation Alpha* (Susan Stoker's world)

ABOUT THE AUTHOR

Contact Me

If stalking an author is your thing and I sure hope it is then here are the links to my social media pages.

If you prefer your stalking to be more intimate, then my group Maddie's Minxes will welcome you with open arms.

General Email: info.maddiewade@gmail.com
Email: maddie@maddiewadeauthor.co.uk
Website: http://www.maddiewadeauthor.co.uk
Facebook page: https://www.facebook.com/maddieuk/
Facebook group: https://www.facebook.com/groups/546325035557882/
Amazon Author page: amazon.com/author/maddiewadeGoodreads: https://www.-goodreads.com/author/show/14854265.Maddie_Wade
Bookbub: https://partners.bookbub.com/authors/3711690/edit
Twitter: @mwadeauthor
Pinterest: @maddie_wade
Instagram: Maddie Author

WANT A FREE SHORT STORY?

Sign up for Maddie's Newsletter using the link below and receive a free copy of the short story, Fortis: Where it all Began.

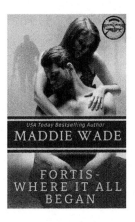

When hard-nosed SAS operator, Zack Cunningham is forced to work a mission with the fiery daughter of the American General, sparks fly. As those heated looks turn into scorching hot stolen kisses, a forbidden love affair begins that neither had expected.

Just as life is looking perfect disaster strikes and Ava Drake is left wondering if she will ever see the man she loves again.

https://dl.bookfunnel.com/cyrjtv3tta

Printed in Great Britain
by Amazon

23179348R00108